Selected Stories by
THOMAS HARDY

Books in this Series:

Selected Stories by O. Henry
Selected Stories by Anton Chekhov
Selected Stories by Guy de Maupassant
Selected Stories by Mark Twain
Selected Stories by Rudyard Kipling
Selected Stories by Leo Tolstoy
Selected Stories by Edgar Allan Poe
Selected Stories by Saki
Selected Stories by Oscar Wilde
Selected Stories by Honoré de Balzac
Selected Stories by Charles Dickens
Selected Stories by D.H. Lawrence
Selected Stories by H.G. Wells
Selected Stories by Jack London
Selected Stories by Joseph Conrad
Selected Stories by Sir Arthur Conan Doyle
Selected Stories by James Joyce
Selected Stories by Virginia Woolf
Selected Stories by Fyodor Dostoyevsky
Selected Stories by Katherine Mansfield
Selected Stories by Wilkie Collins
Selected Stories by Robert Louis Stevenson
Selected Stories by Howard Pyle
Selected Stories by Jerome K. Jerome
Selected Stories by Sir Walter Scott
Selected Stories by H. Rider Haggard
Selected Stories by G.K. Chesterton
Selected Stories by Bram Stoker
Selected Stories by Henry James
Selected Stories by F. Scott Fitzgerald
Selected Stories by W.W. Jacobs
Selected Stories by A.A. Milne
Selected Stories by Nathaniel Hawthorne
Selected Stories by Alexandre Dumas
Selected Essays by Charles Lamb

Selected Stories by
THOMAS HARDY

RUPA

Published by
Rupa Publications India Pvt. Ltd 2014
161-B/4, Gulmohar House,
Yusuf Sarai Community Centre,
New Delhi 110049

Sales centres:
Bengaluru Chennai
Hyderabad Kolkata Mumbai

Selection and Introduction copyright © Terry O'Brien 2014

All rights reserved.
No part of this publication may be reproduced, transmitted,
or stored in a retrieval system, in any form or by any means, electronic,
mechanical, photocopying, recording or otherwise, without the prior
permission of the publisher.

P-ISBN: 978-81-291-3520-9
E-ISBN: 978-93-533-3932-6

Fifth impression 2025

10 9 8 7 6 5

Printed in India

This book is sold subject to the condition that it shall not,
by way of trade or otherwise, be lent, resold, hired out, or otherwise
circulated, without the publisher's prior consent, in any form of binding
or cover other than that in which it is published.

CONTENTS

Introduction   vii

1. An Imaginative Woman   1
2. The Withered Arm   30
3. The Three Strangers   64
4. To Please His Wife   91
5. The Fiddler of the Reels   112
6. The Son's Veto   133
7. For Conscience' Sake   151

INTRODUCTION

Thomas Hardy (2 June 1840–11 January 1928) was an English novelist and poet. Although a Victorian realist like George Eliot, he was highly influenced by Romanticism, especially William Wordsworth. Like Dickens, he was critical of Victorian society, choosing to focus more on the rural way of life. Hardy gained fame as a novelist with *Far from the Madding Crowd* (1874), *The Mayor of Casterbridge* (1886), *Tess of the d'Urbervilles* (1891), and *Jude the Obscure* (1895). His tragic characters generally struggled against their passions and social circumstances. His works were popular subjects for theatre and movies.

- 'An Imaginative Woman' is about Ella Marchmill—an aspiring poet writing under a male pseudonym. The story follows how she finds scraps of poetry written by another man in the holiday lodgings where she and her husband stay, and becomes enamoured with them.
- 'The Withered Arm' is about a milkmaid called Rhoda Brook who bears the illegitimate son of Farmer Lodge.
- 'The Three Strangers' begins with a party of nineteen people assembled in a shepherd's cottage, where they encounter three strangers who have each come to seek shelter for the night.
- 'To Please His Wife' is about a seaman, Shadrach Jolliffe, who returns to his hometown after a long voyage and

ends up involuntarily encouraging the romantic advances of two women, Joanna and Emily. Though he clearly likes Emily more, he ends up marrying Joanna and complex relationships follow.
- 'The Fiddler of the Reels' is the story of Car'line Aspent, who is bewitched and seduced by the dazzling fiddler, Mop Ollamoor. In the process, she rejects her loyal suitor Ned, only to repent her decision and seek him out years later.
- 'The Son's Veto' revolves around the protagonist Sophy, who works as a servant to Reverend Twycott and eventually agrees to his proposal of marriage, despite there being no love between them. After his death, she is proposed to again by Sam Hobson, who had loved her before—but her son Randolph vetoes the proposal.
- 'For Conscience' Sake' begins with Mr Millbourne recounting to his friend Doctor Bindon how he feels troubled for having broken his promise of marriage twenty years previously to a Wessex girl whom he had left with a baby daughter. He wants to rectify the misdeed in some way, so as to restore his sense of self-respect. What follows is the process of rectifying and amending, which leaves one wondering as to how much good it actually does.

1

AN IMAGINATIVE WOMAN

When William Marchmill had finished his inquiries for lodgings at a well-known watering-place of Solentsea in Upper Wessex, he returned to the hotel to find his wife. She, with the children, had rambled along the shore, and Marchmill followed in the direction indicated by the military-looking hall-porter.

'By Jove, how far you've gone! I am quite out of breath,' Marchmill said, rather impatiently, when he came up with his wife, who was reading as she walked, the three children being considerably further ahead with the nurse.

Mrs Marchmill started out of the reverie into which the book had thrown her. 'Yes,' she said, 'you've been such a long time. I was tired of staying in that dreary hotel. But I am sorry if you have wanted me, Will?'

'Well, I have had trouble to suit myself. When you see the airy and comfortable rooms heard of, you find they are stuffy and uncomfortable. Will you come and see if what I've fixed on will do? There is not much room, I am afraid; but I can light on nothing better. The town is rather full.'

The pair left the children and nurse to continue their ramble, and went back together.

In age well-balanced, in personal appearance fairly matched, and in domestic requirements conformable, in temper this couple differed, though even here they did not often clash, he being equable, if not lymphatic, and she decidedly nervous and sanguine. It was to their tastes and fancies, those smallest, greatest particulars, that no common denominator could be applied. Marchmill considered his wife's likes and inclinations somewhat silly; she considered his sordid and material. The husband's business was that of a gunmaker in a thriving city northwards, and his soul was in that business always; the lady was best characterized by that superannuated phrase of elegance 'a votary of the muse'. An impressionable, palpitating creature was Ella, shrinking humanely from detailed knowledge of her husband's trade whenever she reflected that everything he manufactured had for its purpose the destruction of life. She could only recover her equanimity by assuring herself that some, at least, of his weapons were sooner or later used for the extermination of horrid vermin and animals almost as cruel to their inferiors in species as human beings were to theirs.

She had never antecedently regarded this occupation of his as any objection to having him for a husband. Indeed, the necessity of getting life-leased at all cost, a cardinal virtue which all good mothers teach, kept her from thinking of it at all till she had closed with William, had passed the honeymoon, and reached the reflecting stage. Then, like a person who has stumbled upon some object in the dark, she wondered what she had got; mentally walked round it, estimated it; whether it were rare or common; contained gold, silver, or lead; were a clog or a pedestal, everything to her or nothing.

She came to some vague conclusions, and since then had kept her heart alive by pitying her proprietor's obtuseness and want of refinement, pitying herself, and letting off her delicate and ethereal emotions in imaginative occupations, daydreams, and night-sighs, which perhaps would not much have disturbed

William if he had known of them.

Her figure was small, elegant, and slight in build, tripping, or rather bounding, in movement. She was dark-eyed, and had that marvellously bright and liquid sparkle in each pupil which characterizes persons of Ella's cast of soul, and is too often a cause of heartache to the possessor's male friends, ultimately sometimes to herself. Her husband was a tall, long-featured man, with a brown beard; he had a pondering regard; and was, it must be added, usually kind and tolerant to her. He spoke in squarely shaped sentences, and was supremely satisfied with a condition of sublunary things which made weapons a necessity.

Husband and wife walked till they had reached the house they were in search of, which stood in a terrace facing the sea, and was fronted by a small garden of windproof and salt-proof evergreens, stone steps leading up to the porch. It had its number in the row, but, being rather larger than the rest, was in addition sedulously distinguished as Coburg House by its landlady, though everybody else called it 'Thirteen, New Parade'. The spot was bright and lively now; but in winter it became necessary to place sandbags against the door, and to stuff up the keyhole against the wind and rain, which had worn the paint so thin that the priming and knotting showed through.

The householder, who had been watching for the gentleman's return, met them in the passage, and showed the rooms. She informed them that she was a professional man's widow, left in needy circumstances by the rather sudden death of her husband, and she spoke anxiously of the conveniences of the establishment.

Mrs Marchmill said that she liked the situation and the house; but, it being small, there would not be accommodation enough, unless she could have all the rooms.

The landlady mused with an air of disappointment. She wanted the visitors to be her tenants very badly, she said, with obvious honesty. But unfortunately two of the rooms were occupied permanently by a bachelor gentleman. He did not pay season prices, it was true; but as he kept on his apartments all the year round, and was an extremely nice and interesting young man, who gave no trouble, she did not like to turn him out for a month's 'let', even at a high figure. 'Perhaps, however,' she added, 'he might offer to go for a time.'

They would not hear of this, and went back to the hotel, intending to proceed to the agent's to inquire further. Hardly had they sat down to tea when the landlady called. Her gentleman, she said, had been so obliging as to offer to give up his rooms three or four weeks rather than drive the newcomers away.

'It is very kind, but we won't inconvenience him in that way,' said the Marchmills.

'O, it won't inconvenience him, I assure you!' said the landlady eloquently. 'You see, he's a different sort of young man from most—dreamy, solitary, rather melancholy—and he cares more to be here when the southwesterly gales are beating against the door, and the sea washes over the Parade, and there's not a soul in the place, than he does now in the season. He'd just as soon be where, in fact, he's going temporarily to a little cottage on the Island opposite, for a change.' She hoped therefore that they would come.

The Marchmill family accordingly took possession of the house next day, and it seemed to suit them very well. After luncheon Mr Marchmill strolled out towards the pier, and Mrs Marchmill, having despatched the children to their outdoor amusements on the sands, settled herself in more completely, examining this and that article, and testing the reflecting powers of the mirror in the wardrobe door.

In the small back sitting-room, which had been the young bachelor's, she found furniture of a more personal nature than in the rest. Shabby books, of correct rather than rare editions, were piled up in a queerly reserved manner in corners, as if the previous occupant had not conceived the possibility that any incoming person of the season's bringing could care to look inside them. The landlady hovered on the threshold to rectify anything that Mrs Marchmill might not find to her satisfaction.

'I'll make this my own little room,' said the latter, 'because the books are here. By the way, the person who has left seems to have a good many. He won't mind my reading some of them, Mrs Hooper, I hope?'

'O, dear no, ma'am. Yes, he has a good many. You see, he is in the literary line himself somewhat. He is a poet—yes, really a poet—and he has a little income of his own, which is enough to write verses on, but not enough for cutting a figure, even if he cared to.'

'A poet! O, I did not know that.'

Mrs Marchmill opened one of the books, and saw the owner's name written on the title-page. 'Dear me!' she continued; 'I know his name very well—Robert Trewe—of course I do; and his writings! And it is *his* rooms we have taken, and *him* we have turned out of his home?'

Ella Marchmill, sitting down alone a few minutes later, thought with interested surprise of Robert Trewe. Her own latter history will best explain that interest. Herself the only daughter of a struggling man of letters, she had during the last year or two taken to writing poems, in an endeavour to find a congenial channel in which to let flow her painfully embayed emotions, whose former limpidity and sparkle seemed departing in the stagnation caused by the routine of a practical household and the gloom of bearing children to a commonplace father. These poems, subscribed with a masculine pseudonym, had appeared in various obscure magazines, and in two cases in rather prominent ones. In the second of the latter the page which bore her effusion at the bottom, in smallish print, bore at the top, in large print, a few verses on the same subject by this very man, Robert Trewe. Both of them had, in fact, been struck by a tragic incident reported in the daily papers, and had used it simultaneously as an inspiration, the editor remarking in a note upon the coincidence, and that the excellence of both poems prompted him to give them together.

After that event Ella, otherwise 'John Ivy', had watched with much attention the appearance anywhere in print of verse bearing the signature of Robert Trewe, who, with a man's unsusceptibility on the question of sex, had never once thought of passing himself off as a woman. To be sure, Mrs Marchmill had satisfied herself with a sort of reason for doing the contrary in her case; since nobody might believe in her inspiration if they found that the sentiments came from a pushing tradesman's wife, from the mother of three children by a matter-of-fact small-arms manufacturer.

Trewe's verse contrasted with that of the rank and file of recent minor poets in being impassioned rather than ingenious, luxuriant rather than finished. Neither symboliste nor décadent, he was a pessimist in so far as that character applies to a man who looks at the worst contingencies as well as the best in the human condition. Being little attracted by excellences of form and rhythm apart from content, he sometimes, when feeling outran his artistic speed, perpetrated sonnets in the loosely rhymed Elizabethan fashion, which every right-minded reviewer said he ought not to have done.

With sad and hopeless envy, Ella Marchmill had often and often scanned the rival poet's work, so much stronger as it always was than her own feeble lines. She had imitated him, and her inability to touch his level would send her into fits of despondency. Months passed away thus, till she observed from the publishers' list that Trewe had collected his fugitive pieces into a volume, which was duly issued, and was much or little praised according to chance, and had a sale quite sufficient to pay for the printing.

This step onward had suggested to John Ivy the idea of collecting her pieces also, or at any rate of making up a book of her rhymes by adding many in manuscript to the few that had seen the light, for she had been able to get no great number into print. A ruinous charge was made for costs of publication; a few reviews noticed her poor little volume; but nobody talked of it, nobody bought it, and it fell dead in a fortnight—if it had ever been alive.

The author's thoughts were diverted to another groove just then by the discovery that she was going to have a third child, and the collapse of her poetical venture had perhaps less effect upon her mind than it might have done if she had been domestically unoccupied. Her husband had paid the publisher's bill with the doctor's, and there it all had ended for the time. But, though less than a poet of her century, Ella was more than a mere multiplier of her kind, and latterly she had begun to feel the old afflatus once more. And now by an odd conjunction she found herself in the rooms of Robert Trewe.

She thoughtfully rose from her chair and searched the apartment with the interest of a fellow-tradesman. Yes, the volume of his own verse was among the rest. Though quite familiar with its contents, she read it here as if it spoke aloud to her, then called up Mrs Hooper, the landlady, for some trivial service, and inquired again about the young man.

'Well, I'm sure you'd be interested in him, ma'am, if you could see him, only he's so shy that I don't suppose you will.' Mrs Hooper seemed nothing loth to minister to her tenant's curiosity about her predecessor. 'Lived here long? Yes, nearly two years. He keeps on his rooms even when he's not here: the soft air of this place suits his chest, and he likes to be able to come back at any time. He is mostly writing or reading, and doesn't see many people, though, for the matter of that, he is such a good, kind young fellow that folks would only be too glad to be friendly with him if they knew him. You don't meet kind-hearted people every day.'

'Ah, he's kind-hearted...and good.'

'Yes; he'll oblige me in anything if I ask him. "Mr Trewe," I say to him sometimes, "you are rather out of spirits." "Well, I am, Mrs Hooper," he'll say, "though I don't know how you should find it out." "Why not take a little change?" I ask. Then in a day or two he'll say that he will take a trip to Paris, or Norway, or somewhere; and I assure you he comes back all the better for it.'

'Ah, indeed! His is a sensitive nature, no doubt.'

'Yes. Still he's odd in some things. Once when he had finished a poem of his composition late at night he walked up and down the room rehearsing it; and the floors being so thin—jerry-built houses, you know, though I say it myself—he kept me awake up above him till I wished him further... But we get on very well.'

This was but the beginning of a series of conversations about the rising poet as the days went on. On one of these occasions Mrs Hooper drew Ella's attention to what she had not noticed before: minute scribblings in pencil on the wallpaper behind the curtains at the head of the bed.

'O! Let me look,' said Mrs Marchmill, unable to conceal a rush of tender curiosity as she bent her pretty face close to the wall.

'These,' said Mrs Hooper, with the manner of a woman who knew things, 'are the very beginnings and first thoughts of his verses. He has tried to rub most of them out, but you can read them still. My belief is that he wakes up in the night, you know, with some rhyme in his head, and jots it down there on the wall lest he should forget it by the morning. Some of these very lines you see here I have seen afterwards in print in the magazines. Some are newer; indeed, I have not seen that one before. It must have been done only a few days ago.'

'O' yes!...'

Ella Marchmill flushed without knowing why, and suddenly wished her companion would go away, now that the information was imparted. An indescribable consciousness of personal interest rather than literary made her anxious to read the inscription alone; and she accordingly waited till she could do so, with a sense that a great store of emotion would be enjoyed in the act.

Perhaps because the sea was choppy outside the Island, Ella's husband found it much pleasanter to go sailing and steaming about without his wife, who was a bad sailor, than with her. He did not disdain to go thus alone on board the steamboats of the cheap-trippers, where there was dancing by moonlight, and where the couples would come suddenly down with a lurch into each other's arms; for, as he blandly told her, the company was too mixed for him to take her amid such scenes. Thus, while this thriving manufacturer got a great deal of change and sea-air out of his sojourn here, the life, external at least, of Ella was monotonous enough, and mainly consisted in passing a certain number of hours each day in bathing and walking up and down a stretch of shore. But the poetic impulse having again waxed strong, she was possessed by an inner flame which left her hardly conscious of what was proceeding around her.

She had read till she knew by heart Trewe's last little volume of verses, and spent a great deal of time in vainly attempting to rival some of them, till, in her failure, she burst into tears. The personal element in the magnetic attraction exercised by this circumambient, unapproachable master of hers was so much stronger than the intellectual and abstract that she could not understand it. To be sure, she was surrounded noon and night by his customary environment, which literally whispered of him to her at every moment; but he was a man she had never seen, and that all that moved her was the instinct to specialize a waiting emotion on the first fit thing that came to hand did not, of course, suggest itself to Ella.

In the natural way of passion under the too practical conditions which civilization has devised for its fruition, her husband's love for her had not survived, except in the form of fitful friendship, any more than, or even so much as, her own for him; and, being a woman of very living ardours, that required sustenance of some sort, they were beginning to feed on this chancing material, which was, indeed, of a quality far better than chance usually offers.

One day the children had been playing hide-and-seek in a closet, whence, in their excitement, they pulled out some clothing. Mrs Hooper explained that it belonged to Mr Trewe, and hung it up in the closet again. Possessed of her fantasy, Ella went later in the afternoon, when nobody was in that part of the house, opened the closet, unhitched one of the articles, a mackintosh, and put it on, with the waterproof cap belonging to it.

'The mantle of Elijah!' she said. 'Would it might inspire me to rival him, glorious genius that he is!'

Her eyes always grew wet when she thought like that, and she turned to look at herself in the glass. His heart had beat inside that coat, and his brain had worked under that hat at levels of thought she would never reach. The consciousness of her weakness beside him made her feel quite sick. Before she had got the things off her the door opened, and her husband entered the room.

'What the devil—'

She blushed, and removed them.

'I found them in the closet here,' she said, 'and put them on in a freak. What have I else to do? You are always away!'

'Always away? Well...'

That evening she had a further talk with the landlady, who might herself have nourished a half-tender regard for the poet, so ready was she to discourse ardently about him.

'You are interested in Mr Trewe, I know, ma'am,' she said; 'and he has just sent to say that he is going to call tomorrow afternoon to look up some books of his that he wants, if I'll be in, and he may select them from your room?'

'O yes!'

'You could very well meet Mr Trewe then, if you'd like to be in the way!'

She promised with secret delight, and went to bed musing of him.

Next morning her husband observed: 'I've been thinking of what you said, Ell: that I have gone about a good deal and left you without much to amuse you. Perhaps it's true. Today, as there's not much sea, I'll take you with me on board the yacht.'

For the first time in her experience of such an offer Ella was not glad. But she accepted it for the moment. The time for setting out drew near, and she went to get ready. She stood reflecting. The longing to see the poet she was now distinctly in love with overpowered all other considerations.

'I don't want to go,' she said to herself. 'I can't bear to be away! And I won't go.'

She told her husband that she had changed her mind about wishing to sail. He was indifferent, and went his way.

For the rest of the day the house was quiet, the children having gone out upon the sands. The blinds waved in the sunshine to the soft, steady stroke of the sea beyond the wall; and the notes of the Green Silesian band, a troop of foreign gentlemen hired for the season, had drawn almost all the residents and promenaders away from the vicinity of Coburg House. A knock was audible at the door.

Mrs Marchmill did not hear any servant go to answer it, and she became impatient. The books were in the room where she sat; but nobody came up. She rang the bell.

'There is some person waiting at the door,' she said.

'O no, ma'am! He's gone long ago. I answered it.'

Mrs Hooper came in herself.

'So disappointing!' she said. 'Mr Trewe not coming after all!'

'But I heard him knock, I fancy!'

'No; that was somebody inquiring for lodgings who came to the wrong house. I forgot to tell you that Mr Trewe sent a note just before lunch to say I needn't get any tea for him, as he should not require the books, and wouldn't come to select them.'

Ella was miserable, and for a long time could not even reread his mournful ballad on 'Severed Lives,' so aching was her erratic little heart, and so tearful her eyes. When the children came in with wet stockings, and ran up to her to tell her of their adventures, she could not feel that she cared about them half as much as usual.

'Mrs Hooper, have you a photograph of—the gentleman who lived here?' She was getting to be curiously shy in mentioning his name.

'Why, yes. It's in the ornamental frame on the mantelpiece in your own bedroom, ma'am.'

'No; the Royal Duke and Duchess are in that.'

'Yes, so they are; but he's behind them. He belongs rightly to that frame, which I bought on purpose; but as he went away he said: "Cover me up from those strangers that are coming, for God's sake. I don't want them staring at me, and I am sure they won't want me staring at them." So I slipped in the Duke and Duchess temporarily in front of him, as they had no frame, and Royalties are more suitable for letting furnished than a private young man. If you take 'em out you'll see him under. Lord, ma'am, he wouldn't mind if he knew it! He didn't think the next tenant would be such an attractive lady as you, or he wouldn't have thought of hiding himself, perhaps.'

'Is he handsome?' she asked timidly.

'*I* call him so. Some, perhaps, wouldn't.'

'Should I?' she asked, with eagerness.

'I think you would, though some would say he's more striking than handsome; a large-eyed thoughtful fellow, you know, with a very electric flash in his eye when he looks round quickly, such as you'd expect a poet to be who doesn't get his living by it.'

'How old is he?'

'Several years older than yourself, ma'am; about thirty-one or two, I think.'

Ella was, as a matter of fact, a few months over thirty herself; but she did not look nearly so much. Though so immature in nature, she was entering on that tract of life in which emotional women begin to suspect that last love may be stronger than first love; and she would soon, alas, enter on the still more melancholy tract when at least the vainer ones of her sex shrink from receiving a male visitor otherwise than with their backs to the window or the blinds half down. She reflected on Mrs Hooper's remark, and said no more about age.

Just then a telegram was brought up. It came from her husband, who had gone down the Channel as far as Budmouth with his friends in the yacht, and would not be able to get back till next day.

After her light dinner Ella idled about the shore with the

children till dusk, thinking of the yet uncovered photograph in her room, with a serene sense of something ecstatic to come. For, with the subtle luxuriousness of fancy in which this young woman was an adept, on learning that her husband was to be absent that night she had refrained from incontinently rushing upstairs and opening the picture-frame, preferring to reserve the inspection till she could be alone, and a more romantic tinge be imparted to the occasion by silence, candles, solemn sea and stars outside, than was afforded by the garish afternoon sunlight.

The children had been sent to bed, and Ella soon followed, though it was not yet ten o'clock. To gratify her passionate curiosity she now made her preparations, first getting rid of superfluous garments and putting on her dressing-gown, then arranging a chair in front of the table and reading several pages of Trewe's tenderest utterances. Then she fetched the portrait-frame to the light, opened the back, took out the likeness, and set it up before her.

It was a striking countenance to look upon. The poet wore a luxuriant black moustache and imperial, and a slouched hat which shaded the forehead. The large dark eyes described by the landlady showed an unlimited capacity for misery; they looked out from beneath well-shaped brows as if they were reading the universe in the microcosm of the confronter's face, and were not altogether overjoyed at what the spectacle portended.

Ella murmured in her lowest, richest, tenderest tone: 'And it's *you* who've so cruelly eclipsed me these many times!'

As she gazed long at the portrait she fell into thought, till her eyes filled with tears, and she touched the cardboard with her lips. Then she laughed with a nervous lightness, and wiped her eyes.

She thought how wicked she was, a woman having a husband and three children, to let her mind stray to a stranger in this unconscionable manner. No, he was not a stranger! She knew his thoughts and feelings as well as she knew her own; they were, in fact, the self-same thoughts and feelings as hers, which her husband distinctly lacked; perhaps luckily for himself, considering that he had to provide for family expenses.

'He's nearer my real self, he's more intimate with the real me than Will is, after all, even though I've never seen him,' she said.

She laid his book and picture on the table at the bedside, and when she was reclining on the pillow she reread those of Robert Trewe's verses which she had marked from time to time as most touching and true. Putting these aside she set up the photograph on its edge upon the coverlet, and contemplated it as she lay. Then she scanned again by the light of the candle the half-obliterated pencillings on the wallpaper beside her head. There they were—phrases, couplets, bouts-rimes, beginnings and middles of lines, ideas in the rough, like Shelley's scraps, and the least of them so intense, so sweet, so palpitating, that it seemed as if his very breath, warm and loving, fanned her cheeks from those walls, walls that had surrounded his head times and times as they surrounded her own now. He must often have put up his hand so—with the pencil in it. Yes, the writing was sideways, as it would be if executed by one who extended his arm thus.

These inscribed shapes of the poet's world,

'Forms more real than living man,
Nurslings of immortality,'

were, no doubt, the thoughts and spirit-strivings which had come to him in the dead of night, when he could let himself go and have no fear of the frost of criticism. No doubt they had often been written up hastily by the light of the moon, the rays of the lamp, in the blue-grey dawn, in full daylight perhaps never. And now her hair was dragging where his arm had lain when he secured the fugitive fancies; she was sleeping on a poet's lips, immersed in the very essence of him, permeated by his spirit as by an ether.

While she was dreaming the minutes away thus, a footstep came upon the stairs, and in a moment she heard her husband's heavy step on the landing immediately without.

'Ell, where are you?'

What possessed her she could not have described, but, with an instinctive objection to let her husband know what she had been doing, she slipped the photograph under the pillow just as he flung open the door, with the air of a man who had dined not badly.

'O, I beg pardon,' said William Marchmill. 'Have you a headache? I am afraid I have disturbed you.'

'No, I've not got a headache,' said she. 'How is it you've come?'

'Well, we found we could get back in very good time after all, and I didn't want to make another day of it, because of going somewhere else tomorrow.'

'Shall I come down again?'

'O, no. I'm as tired as a dog. I've had a good feed, and I shall turn in straight off. I want to get out at six o'clock tomorrow if I can...I shan't disturb you by my getting up; it will be long before you are awake.' And he came forward into the room.

While her eyes followed his movements, Ella softly pushed the photograph further out of sight.

'Sure you're not ill?' he asked, bending over her.

'No, only wicked!'

'Never mind that.' And he stooped and kissed her. 'I wanted to be with you tonight.'

Next morning Marchmill was called at six o'clock; and in waking and yawning she heard him muttering to himself: 'What the deuce is this that's been crackling under me so?' Imagining her asleep he searched round him and withdrew something. Through her half-opened eyes she perceived it to be Mr Trewe.

'Well, I'm damned!' her husband exclaimed.

'What, dear?' said she.

'O, you are awake? Ha! ha!'

'What *do* you mean?'

'Some bloke's photograph—a friend of our landlady's, I suppose. I wonder how it came here; whisked off the table by accident perhaps when they were making the bed.'

'I was looking at it yesterday, and it must have dropped in then.'

'O, he's a friend of yours? Bless his picturesque heart!'

Ella's loyalty to the object of her admiration could not endure to hear him ridiculed. 'He's a clever man!' she said, with a tremor in her gentle voice which she herself felt to be absurdly uncalled for. 'He is a rising poet—the gentleman who occupied two of these rooms before we came, though I've never seen him.'

'How do you know, if you've never seen him?'

'Mrs Hooper told me when she showed me the photograph.'

'O, well, I must up and be off. I shall be home rather early. Sorry I can't take you today, dear. Mind the children don't go getting drowned.'

That day Mrs Marchmill inquired if Mr Trewe were likely to call at any other time.

'Yes,' said Mrs Hooper. 'He's coming this day week to stay with a friend near here till you leave. He'll be sure to call.'

Marchmill did return quite early in the afternoon; and, opening some letters which had arrived in his absence, declared suddenly that he and his family would have to leave a week earlier than they had expected to do—in short, in three days.

'Surely we can stay a week longer?' she pleaded. 'I like it here.'

'I don't. It is getting rather slow.'

'Then you might leave me and the children!'

'How perverse you are, Ell! What's the use? And have to come to fetch you! No: we'll all return together; and we'll make out our time in North Wales or Brighton a little later on. Besides, you've three days longer yet.'

It seemed to be her doom not to meet the man for whose rival talent she had a despairing admiration, and to whose person she was now absolutely attached. Yet she determined to make a last effort; and having gathered from her landlady that Trewe was living in a lonely spot not far from the fashionable town on the Island opposite, she crossed over in the packet from the neighbouring pier the following afternoon.

What a useless journey it was! Ella knew but vaguely where the house stood, and when she fancied she had found it, and ventured to inquire of a pedestrian if he lived there, the answer returned by the man was that he did not know. And if he did live there, how could she call upon him? Some women might have the assurance to do it, but she had not. How crazy he would think her. She might have asked him to call upon her, perhaps; but she had not the courage for that, either. She lingered mournfully about the picturesque seaside eminence till it was time to return to the town and enter the steamer for recrossing, reaching home for dinner without having been greatly missed.

At the last moment, unexpectedly enough, her husband said that he should have no objection to letting her and the children stay on till the end of the week, since she wished to do so, if she felt herself able to get home without him. She concealed the pleasure this extension of time gave her; and Marchmill went off the next morning alone.

But the week passed, and Trewe did not call.

On Saturday morning the remaining members of the

Marchmill family departed from the place which had been productive of so much fervour in her. The dreary, dreary train; the sun shining in moted beams upon the hot cushions; the dusty permanent way; the mean rows of wire—these things were her accompaniment: while out of the window the deep blue sea-levels disappeared from her gaze, and with them her poet's home. Heavy-hearted, she tried to read, and wept instead.

Mr Marchmill was in a thriving way of business, and he and his family lived in a large new house, which stood in rather extensive grounds a few miles outside the midland city wherein he carried on his trade. Ella's life was lonely here, as the suburban life is apt to be, particularly at certain seasons; and she had ample time to indulge her taste for lyric and elegiac composition. She had hardly got back when she encountered a piece by Robert Trewe in the new number of her favourite magazine, which must have been written almost immediately before her visit to Solentsea, for it contained the very couplet she had seen pencilled on the wallpaper by the bed, and Mrs Hooper had declared to be recent. Ella could resist no longer, but seizing a pen impulsively, wrote to him as a brother-poet, using the name of John Ivy, congratulating him in her letter on his triumphant executions in metre and rhythm of thoughts that moved his soul, as compared with her own brow-beaten efforts in the same pathetic trade.

To this address there came a response in a few days, little as she had dared to hope for it—a civil and brief note, in which the young poet stated that, though he was not well acquainted with Mr Ivy's verse, he recalled the name as being one he had seen attached to some very promising pieces; that he was glad to gain Mr Ivy's acquaintance by letter, and should certainly look with much interest for his productions in the future.

There must have been something juvenile or timid in her own epistle, as one ostensibly coming from a man, she declared to herself; for Trewe quite adopted the tone of an elder and superior in this reply. But what did it matter? He had replied; he had written to her with his own hand from that very room she knew so well, for he was now back again in his quarters.

The correspondence thus begun was continued for two months or more, Ella Marchmill sending him from time to time some that she considered to be the best of her pieces, which he very kindly accepted, though he did not say he sedulously read them, nor did he send her any of his own in return. Ella would have been more hurt at this than she was if she had not known that Trewe laboured under the impression that she was one of his own sex.

Yet the situation was unsatisfactory. A flattering little voice told her that, were he only to see her, matters would be otherwise. No doubt she would have helped on this by making a frank confession of womanhood, to begin with, if something had not happened, to her delight, to render it unnecessary. A friend of her husband's, the editor of the most important newspaper in the city and county, who was dining with them one day, observed during their conversation about the poet that his (the editor's) brother the landscape-painter was a friend of Mr Trewe's, and that the two men were at that very moment in Wales together.

Ella was slightly acquainted with the editor's brother. The next morning down she sat and wrote, inviting him to stay at her house for a short time on his way back, and requesting him to bring with him, if practicable, his companion Mr Trewe, whose acquaintance she was anxious to make. The answer arrived after some few days. Her correspondent and his friend Trewe would have much satisfaction in accepting her invitation on their way southward, which would be on such and such a day in the following week.

Ella was blithe and buoyant. Her scheme had succeeded;

her beloved though as yet unseen one was coming. 'Behold, he standeth behind our wall; he looked forth at the windows, showing himself through the lattice,' she thought ecstatically. 'And, lo, the winter is past, the rain is over and gone, the flowers appear on the earth, the time of the singing of birds is come, and the voice of the turtle is heard in our land.'

But it was necessary to consider the details of lodging and feeding him. This she did most solicitously, and awaited the pregnant day and hour.

It was about five in the afternoon when she heard a ring at the door and the editor's brother's voice in the hall. Poetess as she was, or as she thought herself, she had not been too sublime that day to dress with infinite trouble in a fashionable robe of rich material, having a faint resemblance to the chiton of the Greeks, a style just then in vogue among ladies of an artistic and romantic turn, which had been obtained by Ella of her Bond Street dressmaker when she was last in London. Her visitor entered the drawing-room. She looked towards his rear; nobody else came through the door. Where, in the name of the God of Love, was Robert Trewe?

'O, I'm sorry,' said the painter, after their introductory words had been spoken. 'Trewe is a curious fellow, you know, Mrs Marchmill. He said he'd come; then he said he couldn't. He's rather dusty. We've been doing a few miles with knapsacks, you know; and he wanted to get on home.'

'He—he's not coming?'

'He's not; and he asked me to make his apologies.'

'When did you p-p-part from him?' she asked, her nether lip starting off quivering so much that it was like a tremolo-stop opened in her speech. She longed to run away from this dreadful bore and cry her eyes out.

'Just now, in the turnpike road yonder there.'

'What! He has actually gone past my gates?'

'Yes. When we got to them—handsome gates they are, too, the finest bit of modern wrought-iron work I have seen—when we came to them we stopped, talking there a little while, and then he wished me good-bye and went on. The truth is, he's a little bit depressed just now, and doesn't want to see anybody. He's a very good fellow, and a warm friend, but a little uncertain and gloomy sometimes; he thinks too much of things. His poetry is rather too erotic and passionate, you know, for some tastes; and he has just come in for a terrible slating from the — *Review* that was published yesterday; he saw a copy of it at the station by accident. Perhaps you've read it?'

'No.'

'So much the better. O, it is not worth thinking of; just one of those articles written to order, to please the narrow-minded set of subscribers upon whom the circulation depends. But he's upset by it. He says it is the misrepresentation that hurts him so; that, though he can stand a fair attack, he can't stand lies that he's powerless to refute and stop from spreading. That's just Trewe's weak point. He lives so much by himself that these things affect him much more than they would if he were in the bustle of fashionable or commercial life. So he wouldn't come here, making the excuse that it all looked so new and monied—if you'll pardon—'

'But—he must have known—there was sympathy here! Has he never said anything about getting letters from this address?'

'Yes, yes, he has, from John Ivy—perhaps a relative of yours, he thought, visiting here at the time?'

'Did he—like Ivy, did he say?'

'Well, I don't know that he took any great interest in Ivy.'

'Or in his poems?'

'Or in his poems—so far as I know, that is.'

Robert Trewe took no interest in her house, in her poems, or in their writer. As soon as she could get away she went into the nursery and tried to let off her emotion by unnecessarily kissing the children, till she had a sudden sense of disgust at being reminded how plain-looking they were, like their father.

The obtuse and single-minded landscape-painter never once perceived from her conversation that it was only Trewe she wanted, and not himself. He made the best of his visit, seeming to enjoy the society of Ella's husband, who also took a great fancy to him, and showed him everywhere about the neighbourhood, neither of them noticing Ella's mood.

The painter had been gone only a day or two when, while sitting upstairs alone one morning, she glanced over the London paper just arrived, and read the following paragraph:—

'SUICIDE OF A POET

'Mr Robert Trewe, who has been favourably known for some years as one of our rising lyrists, committed suicide at his lodgings at Solentsea on Saturday evening last by shooting himself in the right temple with a revolver. Readers hardly need to be reminded that Mr Trewe has recently attracted the attention of a much wider public than had hitherto known him, by his new volume of verse, mostly of an impassioned kind, entitled "Lyrics to a Woman Unknown", which has been already favourably noticed in these pages for the extraordinary gamut of feeling it traverses, and which has been made the subject of a severe, if not ferocious, criticism in the—*Review*. It is supposed, though not certainly known, that the article may have partially conduced to the sad act, as a copy of the review in question was found on his writing-table; and he has been observed to be in a somewhat depressed state of mind since the critique appeared.'

Then came the report of the inquest, at which the following letter was read, it having been addressed to a friend at a distance:

> 'DEAR—, Before these lines reach your hands I shall be delivered from the inconveniences of seeing, hearing, and knowing more of the things around me. I will not trouble you by giving my reasons for the step I have taken, though I can assure you they were sound and logical. Perhaps had I been blessed with a mother, or a sister, or a female friend of another sort tenderly devoted to me, I might have thought it worth while to continue my present existence. I have long dreamt of such an unattainable creature, as you know, and she, this undiscoverable, elusive one, inspired my last volume; the imaginary woman alone, for, in spite of what has been said in some quarters, there is no real woman behind the title. She has continued to the last unrevealed, unmet, unwon. I think it desirable to mention this in order that no blame may attach to any real woman as having been the cause of my decease by cruel or cavalier treatment of me. Tell my landlady that I am sorry to have caused her this unpleasantness; but my occupancy of the rooms will soon be forgotten. There are ample funds in my name at the bank to pay all expenses.—R. TREWE.'

Ella sat for a while as if stunned, then rushed into the adjoining chamber and flung herself upon her face on the bed.

Her grief and distraction shook her to pieces; and she lay in this frenzy of sorrow for more than an hour. Broken words came every now and then from her quivering lips: 'O, if he had only known of me—known of me—me!...O, if I had only once met him—only once; and put my hand upon his hot forehead—kissed him—let him know how I loved him—that I would have suffered shame and scorn, would have lived and died, for him!

Perhaps it would have saved his dear life!... But no—it was not allowed! God is a jealous God; and that happiness was not for him and me!'

All possibilities were over; the meeting was stultified. Yet it was almost visible to her in her fantasy even now, though it could never be substantiated.

'The hour which might have been, yet might not be,
Which man's and woman's heart conceived and bore,
Yet whereof life was barren.'

◆

She wrote to the landlady at Solentsea in the third person, in as subdued a style as she could command, enclosing a postal order for a sovereign, and informing Mrs Hooper that Mrs Marchmill had seen in the papers the sad account of the poet's death, and having been, as Mrs Hooper was aware, much interested in Mr Trewe during her stay at Coburg House, she would be obliged if Mrs Hooper could obtain a small portion of his hair before his coffin was closed down, and send it her as a memorial of him, as also the photograph that was in the frame.

By the return post a letter arrived containing what had been requested. Ella wept over the portrait and secured it in her private drawer; the lock of hair she tied with white ribbon and put in her bosom, whence she drew it and kissed it every now and then in some unobserved nook.

'What's the matter?' said her husband, looking up from his newspaper on one of these occasions. 'Crying over something? A lock of hair? Whose is it?'

'He's dead!' she murmured.

'Who?'

'I don't want to tell you, Will, just now, unless you insist!' she said, a sob hanging heavy in her voice.

'O, all right.'

'Do you mind my refusing? I will tell you some day.'

'It doesn't matter in the least, of course.'

He walked away whistling a few bars of no tune in particular; and when he had got down to his factory in the city the subject came into Marchmill's head again.

He, too, was aware that a suicide had taken place recently at the house they had occupied at Solentsea. Having seen the volume of poems in his wife's hand of late, and heard fragments of the landlady's conversation about Trewe when they were her tenants, he all at once said to himself, 'Why of course it's he! How the devil did she get to know him? What sly animals women are!'

Then he placidly dismissed the matter, and went on with his daily affairs. By this time Ella at home had come to a determination. Mrs Hooper, in sending the hair and photograph, had informed her of the day of the funeral; and as the morning and noon wore on an overpowering wish to know where they were laying him took possession of the sympathetic woman. Caring very little now what her husband or anyone else might think of her eccentricities, she wrote Marchmill a brief note, stating that she was called away for the afternoon and evening, but would return on the following morning. This she left on his desk, and having given the same information to the servants, went out of the house on foot.

When Mr Marchmill reached home early in the afternoon the servants looked anxious. The nurse took him privately aside, and hinted that her mistress's sadness during the past few days had been such that she feared she had gone out to drown herself. Marchmill reflected. Upon the whole he thought that she had not done that. Without saying whither he was bound he also started off, telling them not to sit up for him. He drove to the railway-station, and took a ticket for Solentsea.

It was dark when he reached the place, though he had come

by a fast train, and he knew that if his wife had preceded him thither it could only have been by a slower train, arriving not a great while before his own. The season at Solentsea was now past: the parade was gloomy, and the flys were few and cheap. He asked the way to the Cemetery, and soon reached it. The gate was locked, but the keeper let him in, declaring, however, that there was nobody within the precincts. Although it was not late, the autumnal darkness had now become intense; and he found some difficulty in keeping to the serpentine path which led to the quarter where, as the man had told him, the one or two interments for the day had taken place. He stepped upon the grass, and, stumbling over some pegs, stooped now and then to discern if possible a figure against the sky. He could see none; but lighting on a spot where the soil was trodden, beheld a crouching object beside a newly made grave. She heard him, and sprang up.

'Ell, how silly this is!' he said indignantly. 'Running away from home—I never heard such a thing! Of course I am not jealous of this unfortunate man; but it is too ridiculous that you, a married woman with three children and a fourth coming, should go losing your head like this over a dead lover!... Do you know you were locked in? You might not have been able to get out all night.'

She did not answer.

'I hope it didn't go far between you and him, for your own sake.'

'Don't insult me, Will.'

'Mind, I won't have any more of this sort of thing; do you hear?'

'Very well,' she said.

He drew her arm within his own, and conducted her out of the Cemetery. It was impossible to get back that night; and not wishing to be recognized in their present sorry condition, he took her to a miserable little coffee-house close to the station, whence they departed early in the morning, travelling almost without speaking, under the sense that it was one of those dreary situations occurring in married life which words could not mend, and reaching their own door at noon.

The months passed, and neither of the twain ever ventured to start a conversation upon this episode. Ella seemed to be only too frequently in a sad and listless mood, which might almost have been called pining. The time was approaching when she would have to undergo the stress of childbirth for a fourth time, and that apparently did not tend to raise her spirits.

'I don't think I shall get over it this time!' she said one day.

'Pooh! what childish foreboding! Why shouldn't it be as well now as ever?'

She shook her head. 'I feel almost sure I am going to die; and I should be glad, if it were not for Nelly, and Frank, and Tiny.'

'And me!'

'You'll soon find somebody to fill my place,' she murmured, with a sad smile. 'And you'll have a perfect right to; I assure you of that.'

'Ell, you are not thinking still about that—poetical friend of yours?'

She neither admitted nor denied the charge. 'I am not going to get over my illness this time,' she reiterated. 'Something tells me I shan't.'

This view of things was rather a bad beginning, as it usually is; and, in fact, six weeks later, in the month of May, she was lying in her room, pulseless and bloodless, with hardly strength enough left to follow up one feeble breath with another, the infant for whose unnecessary life she was slowly parting with her own being fat and well. Just before her death she spoke to Marchmill softly:

'Will, I want to confess to you the entire circumstances of that—about you know what—that time we visited Solentsea. I can't tell what possessed me—how I could forget you so, my husband! But I had got into a morbid state: I thought you had been unkind; that you had neglected me; that you weren't up to my intellectual level, while he was, and far above it. I wanted a fuller appreciator, perhaps, rather than another lover—'

She could get no further then for very exhaustion; and she went off in sudden collapse a few hours later, without having said anything more to her husband on the subject of her love for the poet. William Marchmill, in truth, like most husbands of several years' standing, was little disturbed by retrospective jealousies, and had not shown the least anxiety to press her for confessions concerning a man dead and gone beyond any power of inconveniencing him more.

But when she had been buried a couple of years it chanced one day that, in turning over some forgotten papers that he wished to destroy before his second wife entered the house, he lighted on a lock of hair in an envelope, with the photograph of the deceased poet, a date being written on the back in his late wife's hand. It was that of the time they spent at Solentsea.

Marchmill looked long and musingly at the hair and portrait, for something struck him. Fetching the little boy who had been the death of his mother, now a noisy toddler, he took him on his knee, held the lock of hair against the child's head, and set up the photograph on the table behind, so that he could closely compare the features each countenance presented. There were undoubtedly strong traces of resemblance; the dreamy and peculiar expression of the poet's face sat, as the transmitted idea, upon the child's, and the hair was of the same hue.

'I'm damned if I didn't think so!' murmured Marchmill. 'Then she did play me false with that fellow at the lodgings! Let me see: the dates—the second week in August...the third week in May...Yes...yes...Get away, you poor little brat! You are nothing to me!'

2

THE WITHERED ARM

I
A Lorn Milkmaid

It was an eighty-cow dairy, and the troop of milkers, regular and supernumerary, were all at work; for, though the time of year was as yet but early April, the feed lay entirely in water-meadows, and the cows were 'in full pail'. The hour was about six in the evening, and three-fourths of the large, red, rectangular animals having been finished off, there was opportunity for a little conversation.

'He do bring home his bride tomorrow, I hear. They've come as far as Anglebury today.'

The voice seemed to proceed from the belly of the cow called Cherry, but the speaker was a milking-woman, whose face was buried in the flank of that motionless beast.

'Hav' anybody seen her?' said another.

There was a negative response from the first. 'Though they say she's a rosy-cheeked, tisty-tosty little body enough,' she added; and as the milkmaid spoke she turned her face so that she could glance past her cow's tail to the other side of the barton, where a thin, fading woman of thirty milked somewhat apart from the rest.

'Years younger than he, they say,' continued the second, with also a glance of reflectiveness in the same direction.

'How old do you call him, then?'

'Thirty or so.'

'More like forty,' broke in an old milkman near, in a long white pinafore or 'wropper', and with the brim of his hat tied down, so that he looked like a woman. 'A was born before our Great Weir was built, and I hadn't man's wages when I laved water there.'

The discussion waxed so warm that the purr of the milk-streams became jerky, till a voice from another cow's belly cried with authority, 'Now then, what the Turk do it matter to us about Farmer Lodge's age, or Farmer Lodge's new mis'ess? I shall have to pay him nine pound a year for the rent of every one of these milchers, whatever his age or hers. Get on with your work, or 'twill be dark afore we have done. The evening is pinking in a'ready.' This speaker was the dairyman himself, by whom the milkmaids and men were employed.

Nothing more was said publicly about Farmer Lodge's wedding, but the first woman murmured under her cow to her next neighbour. ''Tis hard for she,' signifying the thin worn milkmaid aforesaid.

'O no,' said the second. 'He ha'n't spoke to Rhoda Brook for years.'

When the milking was done they washed their pails and hung them on a many-forked stand made as usual of the peeled limb of an oak-tree, set upright in the earth, and resembling a colossal antlered horn. The majority then dispersed in various directions homeward. The thin woman who had not spoken was joined by a boy of twelve or thereabout, and the twain went away up the field also.

Their course lay apart from that of the others, to a lonely spot high above the water-meads, and not far from the border of Egdon Heath, whose dark countenance was visible in the distance as they drew nigh to their home.

'They've just been saying down in barton that your father brings his young wife home from Anglebury tomorrow,' the woman observed. 'I shall want to send you for a few things to market, and you'll be pretty sure to meet 'em.'

'Yes, Mother,' said the boy. 'Is Father married then?'

'Yes... You can give her a look, and tell me what she's like, if you do see her.'

'Yes, Mother.'

'If she's dark or fair, and if she's tall—as tall as I. And if she seems like a woman who has ever worked for a living, or one that has been always well off, and has never done anything, and shows marks of the lady on her, as I expect she do.'

'Yes.'

They crept up the hill in the twilight and entered the cottage. It was built of mud walls, the surface of which had been washed by many rains into channels and depressions that left none of the original flat face visible, while here and there in the thatch above a rafter showed like a bone protruding through the skin.

She was kneeling down in the chimney-corner, before two pieces of turf laid together with the heather inwards, blowing at the red-hot ashes with her breath till the turves flamed. The radiance lit her pale cheek, and made her dark eyes, that had once been handsome, seem handsome anew. 'Yes,' she resumed, 'see if she is dark or fair, and if you can, notice if her hands be white; if not, see if they look as though she had ever done housework, or are milker's hands like mine.'

The boy again promised, inattentively this time, his mother not observing that he was cutting a notch with his pocket-knife in the beech-backed chair.

II
The Young Wife

The road from Anglebury to Holmstoke is in general level, but there is one place where a sharp ascent breaks its monotony. Farmers homeward-bound from the former market-town, who trot all the rest of the way, walk their horses up this short incline.

The next evening while the sun was yet bright a handsome new gig, with a lemon-coloured body and red wheels, was spinning westward along the level highway at the heels of a powerful mare. The driver was a yeoman in the prime of life, cleanly shaven like an actor, his face being toned to that bluish-vermilion hue which so often graces a thriving farmer's features when returning home after successful dealings in the town. Beside him sat a woman, many years his junior—almost, indeed, a girl. Her face too was fresh in colour, but it was of a totally different quality—soft and evanescent, like the light under a heap of rose-petals.

Few people travelled this way, for it was not a main road; and the long white riband of gravel that stretched before them was empty, save of one small scarce-moving speck, which presently resolved itself into the figure of a boy, who was creeping on at a snail's pace, and continually looking behind him—the heavy bundle he carried being some excuse for, if not the reason of, his dilatoriness. When the bouncing gig-party slowed at the bottom of the incline above mentioned, the pedestrian was only a few yards in front. Supporting the large bundle by putting one hand on his hip, he turned and looked straight at the farmer's wife as though he would read her through and through, pacing along abreast of the horse.

The low sun was full in her face, rendering every feature, shade, and colour distinct, from the curve of her little nostril to the colour of her eyes. The farmer, though he seemed annoyed at the boy's persistent presence, did not order him to get out of the way; and thus the lad preceded them, his hard gaze never leaving her, till they reached the top of the ascent, when the farmer trotted on with relief in his lineaments having taken no outward notice of the boy whatever.

'How that poor lad stared at me!' said the young wife.

'Yes, dear; I saw that he did.'

'He is one of the village, I suppose?'

'One of the neighbourhood. I think he lives with his mother a mile or two off.'

'He knows who we are, no doubt?'

'O yes. You must expect to be stared at just at first, my pretty Gertrude.'

'I do,—though I think the poor boy may have looked at us in the hope we might relieve him of his heavy load, rather than from curiosity.'

'O no,' said her husband offhandedly. 'These country lads will carry a hundredweight once they get it on their backs; besides his pack had more size than weight in it. Now, then, another mile and I shall be able to show you our house in the distance—if it is not too dark before we get there.' The wheels spun round, and particles flew from their periphery as before, till a white house of ample dimensions revealed itself, with farm-buildings and ricks at the back.

Meanwhile the boy had quickened his pace, and turning up a by-lane some mile-and-a-half short of the white farmstead, ascended towards the leaner pastures, and so on to the cottage of his mother.

She had reached home after her day's milking at the outlying dairy, and was washing cabbage at the doorway in the declining light. 'Hold up the net a moment,' she said, without preface, as the boy came up.

He flung down his bundle, held the edge of the cabbage-net, and as she filled its meshes with the dripping leaves she went on, 'Well, did you see her?'

'Yes; quite plain.'

'Is she ladylike?'

'Yes; and more. A lady complete.'

'Is she young?'

'Well, she's growed up, and her ways be quite a woman's.'

'Of course. What colour is her hair and face?'

'Her hair is lightish, and her face as comely as a live doll's.'

'Her eyes, then, are not dark like mine?'

'No—of a bluish turn, and her mouth is very nice and red; and when she smiles, her teeth show white.'

'Is she tall?' said the woman sharply.

'I couldn't see. She was sitting down.'

'Then do you go to Holmstoke church tomorrow morning: she's sure to be there. Go early and notice her walking in, and come home and tell me if she's taller than I.'

'Very well, Mother. But why don't you go and see for yourself?'

'*I* go to see her! I wouldn't look up at her if she were to pass my window this instant. She was with Mr Lodge, of course. What did he say or do?'

'Just the same as usual.'

'Took no notice of you?'

'None.'

Next day the mother put a clean shirt on the boy, and started him off for Holmstoke church. He reached the ancient little pile when the door was just being opened, and he was the first to enter. Taking his seat by the font, he watched all the parishioners file in. The well-to-do Farmer Lodge came nearly last; and his young wife, who accompanied him, walked up the aisle with the shyness natural to a modest woman who had appeared thus for the first time. As all other eyes were fixed upon her, the youth's stare was not noticed now.

When he reached home his mother said, 'Well?' before he had entered the room.

'She is not tall. She is rather short,' he replied.

'Ah!' said his mother, with satisfaction.

'But she's very pretty—very. In fact, she's lovely.'

The youthful freshness of the yeoman's wife had evidently made an impression even on the somewhat hard nature of the boy.

'That's all I want to hear,' said his mother quickly. 'Now, spread the tablecloth. The hare you wired is very tender; but mind nobody catches you. You've never told me what sort of hands she had.'

'I have never seen 'em. She never took off her gloves.'

'What did she wear this morning?'

'A white bonnet and a silver-coloured gownd. It whewed and whistled so loud when it rubbed against the pews that the lady coloured up more than ever for very shame at the noise, and pulled it in to keep it from touching; but when she pushed into her seat, it whewed more than ever. Mr Lodge, he seemed pleased, and his waistcoat stuck out, and his great golden seals hung like a lord's; but she seemed to wish her noisy gownd anywhere but on her.'

'Not she! However, that will do now.'

These descriptions of the newly-married couple were continued from time to time by the boy at his mother's request, after any chance encounter he had had with them. But Rhoda Brook, though she might easily have seen young Mrs Lodge for herself by walking a couple of miles, would never attempt an excursion towards the quarter where the farmhouse lay. Neither did she, at the daily milking in the dairyman's yard on Lodge's outlying second farm, ever speak on the subject of the recent marriage. The dairyman, who rented the cows of Lodge, and knew perfectly the tall milkmaid's history, with manly kindness always kept the gossip in the cow-barton from annoying Rhoda. But the atmosphere thereabout was full of the subject the first days of Mrs Lodge's arrival; and from her boy's description and the casual words of the other milkers, Rhoda Brook could raise a mental image of the unconscious Mrs Lodge that was realistic as a photograph.

III
A Vision

One night, two or three weeks after the bridal return, when the boy had gone to bed, Rhoda sat a long time over the turf ashes that she had raked out in front of her to extinguish them. She contemplated so intently the new wife, as presented to her in her mind's eye over the embers, that she forgot the lapse of time. At last, wearied by her day's work, she too retired.

But the figure which had occupied her so much during this and the previous days was not to be banished at night. For the first time Gertrude Lodge visited the supplanted woman in her dreams. Rhoda Brook dreamed—since her assertion that she really saw, before falling asleep, was not to be believed—that the young wife, in the pale silk dress and white bonnet, but with features shockingly distorted, and wrinkled as by age, was sitting upon her chest as she lay. The pressure of Mrs Lodge's person grew heavier; the blue eyes peered cruelly into her face: and then the figure thrust forward its left hand mockingly, so as to make the wedding-ring it wore glitter in Rhoda's eyes. Maddened mentally, and nearly suffocated by pressure, the sleeper struggled; the incubus, still regarding her, withdrew to the foot of the bed, only, however, to come forward by degrees, resume her seat, and flash her left hand as before.

Gasping for breath, Rhoda, in a last desperate effort, swung out her right hand, seized the confronting spectre by its obtrusive left arm, and whirled it backward to the floor, starting up herself as she did so with a low cry.

'O, merciful heaven!' she cried, sitting on the edge of the bed in a cold sweat; 'that was not a dream—she was here!'

She could feel her antagonist's arm within her grasp even now—the very flesh and bone of it, as it seemed. She looked on the floor whither she had whirled the spectre, but there was nothing to be seen.

Rhoda Brook slept no more that night, and when she went milking at the next dawn they noticed how pale and haggard she looked. The milk that she drew quivered into the pail; her hand had not calmed even yet, and still retained the feel of the arm. She came home to breakfast as wearily as if it had been supper-time.

'What was that noise in your chimmer, mother, last night?' said her son. 'You fell off the bed, surely?'

'Did you hear anything fall? At what time?'

'Just when the clock struck two.'

She could not explain, and when the meal was done went silently about her household work, the boy assisting her, for he hated going afield on the farms, and she indulged his reluctance. Between eleven and twelve the garden-gate clicked, and she lifted her eyes to the window. At the bottom of the garden, within the gate, stood the woman of her vision. Rhoda seemed transfixed.

'Ah, she said she would come!' exclaimed the boy, also observing her.

'Said so—when? How does she know us?'

'I have seen and spoken to her. I talked to her yesterday.'

'I told you,' said the mother, flushing indignantly, 'never to speak to anybody in that house, or go near the place.'

'I did not speak to her till she spoke to me. And I did not

go near the place. I met her in the road.'

'What did you tell her?'

'Nothing. She said, "Are you the poor boy who had to bring the heavy load from market?" And she looked at my boots, and said they would not keep my feet dry if it came on wet, because they were so cracked. I told her I lived with my mother, and we had enough to do to keep ourselves, and that's how it was; and she said then: "I'll come and bring you some better boots, and see your mother." She gives away things to other folks in the meads besides us.'

Mrs Lodge was by this time close to the door—not in her silk, as Rhoda had dreamt of in the bedchamber, but in a morning hat, and gown of common light material, which became her better than silk. On her arm she carried a basket.

The impression remaining from the night's experience was still strong. Rhoda had almost expected to see the wrinkles, the scorn and the cruelty on her visitor's face.

She would have escaped an interview, had escape been possible. There was, however, no back door to the cottage, and in an instant the boy had lifted the latch to Mrs Lodge's gentle knock.

'I see I have come to the right house,' said she, glancing at the lad, and smiling. 'But I was not sure till you opened the door.'

The figure and action were those of the phantom; but her voice was so indescribably sweet, her glance so winning, her smile so tender, so unlike that of Rhoda's midnight visitant, that the latter could hardly believe the evidence of her senses. She was truly glad that she had not hidden away in sheer aversion, as she had been inclined to do. In her basket Mrs Lodge brought the pair of boots that she had promised to the boy, and other useful articles.

At these proofs of a kindly feeling towards her and hers Rhoda's heart reproached her bitterly. This innocent young thing should have her blessing and not her curse. When she left them a light seemed gone from the dwelling. Two days later she came again to know if the boots fitted; and less than a fortnight after paid Rhoda another call. On this occasion the boy was absent.

'I walk a good deal,' said Mrs Lodge, 'and your house is the nearest outside our own parish. I hope you are well. You don't look quite well.'

Rhoda said she was well enough; and, indeed, though the paler of the two, there was more of the strength that endures in her well-defined features and large frame than in the soft-cheeked young woman before her. The conversation became quite confidential as regarded their powers and weaknesses; and when Mrs Lodge was leaving, Rhoda said, 'I hope you will find this air agree with you, ma'am, and not suffer from the damp of the water-meads.'

The younger one replied that there was not much doubt of it, her general health being usually good. 'Though, now you remind me, she added, 'I have one little ailment which puzzles me. It is nothing serious, but I cannot make it out.'

She uncovered her left hand and arm; and their outline confronted Rhoda's gaze as the exact original of the limb she had beheld and seized in her dream. Upon the pink round surface of the arm were faint marks of an unhealthy colour, as if produced by a rough grasp. Rhoda's eyes became riveted on the discolourations; she fancied that she discerned in them the shape of her own four fingers.

'How did it happen?' she said mechanically.

'I cannot tell,' replied Mrs Lodge, shaking her head. 'One night when I was sound asleep, dreaming I was away in some strange place, a pain suddenly shot into my arm there, and was so keen as to awaken me. I must have struck it in the daytime, I suppose, though I don't remember doing so.' She added, laughing, 'I tell my dear husband that it looks just as if he had flown into a rage and struck me there. O, I daresay it will soon disappear.'

'Ha, ha! Yes... On what night did it come?'

Mrs Lodge considered, and said it would be a fortnight ago on the morrow. 'When I awoke I could not remember where I was,' she added, 'till the clock striking two reminded me.'

She had named the night and hour of Rhoda's spectral encounter, and Rhoda felt like a guilty thing. The artless disclosure startled her; she did not reason on the freaks of coincidence; and all the scenery of that ghastly night returned with double vividness to her mind.

'O, can it be,' she said to herself, when her visitor had departed, 'that I exercise a malignant power over people against my own will?' She knew that she had been slyly called a witch since her fall; but never having understood why that particular stigma had been attached to her, it had passed disregarded. Could this be the explanation, and had such things as this ever happened before?

IV

A Suggestion

The summer drew on, and Rhoda Brook almost dreaded to meet Mrs Lodge again, notwithstanding that her feeling for the young wife amounted well-nigh to affection. Something in her own individuality seemed to convict Rhoda of crime. Yet a fatality sometimes would direct the steps of the latter to the outskirts of Holmstoke whenever she left her house for any other purpose than her daily work; and hence it happened that their next encounter was out of doors. Rhoda could not avoid the subject which had so mystified her, and after the first few words she stammered, 'I hope your—arm is well again, ma'am?' She had perceived with consternation that Gertrude

Lodge carried her left arm stiffly.

'No; it not quite well. Indeed it is no better at all; it is rather worse. It pains me dreadfully sometimes.'

'Perhaps you had better go to a doctor, ma'am.'

She replied that she had already seen a doctor. Her husband had insisted upon her going to one. But the surgeon had not seemed to understand the afflicted limb at all; he had told her to bathe it in hot water, and she had bathed it, but the treatment had done no good.

'Will you let me see it?' said the milkwoman.

Mrs Lodge pushed up her sleeve and disclosed the place, which was a few inches above the wrist. As soon as Rhoda Brook saw it, she could hardly preserve her composure. There was nothing of the nature of a wound, but the arm at that point had a shrivelled look, and the outline of the four fingers appeared more distinct than at the former time. Moreover, she fancied that they were imprinted in precisely the relative position of her clutch upon the arm in the trance; the first finger towards Gertrude's wrist, and the fourth towards her elbow.

What the impress resembled seemed to have struck Gertrude herself since their last meeting. 'It looks almost like finger-marks,' she said; adding with a faint laugh, 'my husband says it is as if some witch, or the devil himself, had taken hold of me there, and blasted the flesh.'

Rhoda shivered. 'That's fancy,' she said hurriedly. 'I wouldn't mind it, if I were you.'

'I shouldn't so much mind it,' said the younger, with hesitation, 'if—if I hadn't a notion that it makes my husband dislike me—no, love me less. Men think so much of personal appearance.'

'Some do—he for one.'

'Yes; and he was very proud of mine, at first.'

'Keep your arm covered from his sight.'

'Ah—he knows the disfigurement is there!' She tried to hide the tears that filled her eyes.

'Well, ma'am, I earnestly hope it will go away soon.'

And so the milkwoman's mind was chained anew to the subject by a horrid sort of spell as she returned home. The sense of having been guilty of an act of malignity increased, affect as she might to ridicule her superstition. In her secret heart Rhoda did not altogether object to a slight diminution of her successor's beauty, by whatever means it had come about; but she did not wish to inflict upon her physical pain. For though this pretty young woman had rendered impossible any reparation which Lodge might have made Rhoda for his past conduct, everything like resentment at the unconscious usurpation had quite passed away from the elder's mind.

If the sweet and kindly Gertrude Lodge only knew of the dream-scene in the bedchamber, what would she think? Not to inform her of it seemed treachery in the presence of her friendliness; but tell she could not of her own accord—neither could she devise a remedy.

She mused upon the matter the greater part of the night; and the next day, after the morning milking, set out to obtain another glimpse of Gertrude Lodge if she could, being held to her by a gruesome fascination. By watching the house from a distance the milkmaid was presently able to discern the farmer's wife in a ride she was taking alone—probably to join her husband in some distant field. Mrs Lodge perceived her, and cantered in her direction.

'Good morning, Rhoda!' Gertrude said, when she had come up. 'I was going to call.'

Rhoda noticed that Mrs Lodge held the reins with some difficulty.

'I hope—the bad arm,' said Rhoda.

'They tell me there is possibly one way by which I might

be able to find out the cause, and so perhaps the cure of it,' replied the other anxiously. 'It is by going to some clever man over in Egdon Heath. They did not know if he was still alive—and I cannot remember his name at this moment; but they said that you knew more of his movements than anybody else hereabout, and could tell me if he were still to be consulted. Dear me—what was his name? But you know.'

'Not Conjuror Trendle?' said her thin companion, turning pale.

'Trendle—yes. Is he alive?'

'I believe so,' said Rhoda, with reluctance.

'Why do you call him conjuror?'

'Well—they say—they used to say he was a—he had powers other folks have not.'

'O, how could my people be so superstitious as to recommend a man of that sort! I thought they meant some medical man. I shall think no more of him.'

Rhoda looked relieved, and Mrs Lodge rode on. The milkwoman had inwardly seen, from the moment she heard of her having been mentioned as a reference for this man, that there must exist a sarcastic feeling among the work-folk that a sorceress would know the whereabouts of the exorcist. They suspected her, then. A short time ago this would have given no concern to a woman of her common sense. But she had a haunting reason to be superstitious now; and she had been seized with sudden dread that this Conjuror Trendle might name her as the malignant influence which was blasting the fair person of Gertrude, and so lead her friend to hate her for ever, and to treat her as some fiend in human shape.

But all was not over. Two days after, a shadow intruded into the window-pattern thrown on Rhoda Brook's floor by the afternoon sun. The woman opened the door at once, almost breathlessly.

'Are you alone?' said Gertrude. She seemed to be no less harassed and anxious than Rhoda herself.

'Yes,' said Rhoda.

'The place on my arm seems worse, and troubles me!' the young farmer's wife went on. 'It is so mysterious! I do hope it will not be an incurable wound. I have again been thinking of what they said about Conjuror Trendle. I don't really believe in such men, but I should not mind just visiting him, from curiosity—though on no account must my husband know. Is it far to where he lives?'

'Yes—five miles,' said Rhoda backwardly. 'In the heart of Egdon.'

'Well, I should have to walk. Could not you go with me to show me the way—say tomorrow afternoon?'

'O, not I; that is—,' the milkwoman murmured, with a start of dismay. Again the dread seized her that something to do with her fierce act in the dream might be revealed, and her character in the eyes of the most useful friend she had ever had be ruined irretrievably.

Mrs Lodge urged, and Rhoda finally assented, though with much misgiving. Sad as the journey would be to her, she could not conscientiously stand in the way of a possible remedy for her patron's strange affliction. It was agreed that, to escape suspicion of their mystic intent, they should meet at the edge of the heath at the corner of a plantation which was visible from the spot where they now stood.

V

Conjuror Trendle

By the next afternoon Rhoda would have done anything to escape this inquiry. But she had promised to go. Moreover, there was a horrid fascination at times in becoming instrumental in throwing such possible light on her own character as would reveal her to be something greater in the occult world than she had ever herself suspected.

She started just before the time of day mentioned between them, and half an hour's brisk walking brought her to the southeastern extension of the Egdon tract of country, where the fir plantation was. A slight figure, cloaked and veiled, was already there. Rhoda recognized, almost with a shudder, that Mrs Lodge bore her left arm in a sling.

They hardly spoke to each other, and immediately set out on their climb into the interior of this solemn country, which stood high above the rich alluvial soil they had left half an hour before. It was a long walk; thick clouds made the atmosphere dark, though it was as yet only early afternoon; and the wind howled dismally over the slopes of the heath—not improbably the same heath which had witnessed the agony of the Wessex King Ina, presented to after-ages as Lear. Gertrude Lodge talked most, Rhoda replying with monosyllabic preoccupation. She had a strange dislike to walking on the side of her companion where hung the afflicted arm, moving round to the other when inadvertently near it. Much heather had been brushed by their feet when they descended upon a cart-track, beside which stood the house of the man they sought.

He did not profess his remedial practices openly, or care anything about their continuance, his direct interests being those of a dealer in furze, turf, 'sharp sand', and other local products. Indeed, he affected not to believe largely in his own powers, and when warts that had been shown him for cure miraculously disappeared—which it must be owned they infallibly did—he would say lightly, 'O, I only drink a glass of grog upon 'em at your expense—perhaps it's all chance,' and immediately turn the subject.

He was at home when they arrived, having in fact seen

them descending into his valley. He was a grey-bearded man, with a reddish face, and he looked singularly at Rhoda the first moment he beheld her. Mrs Lodge told him her errand; and then with words of self-disparagement he examined her arm.

'Medicine can't cure it,' he said promptly. ''Tis the work of an enemy.'

Rhoda shrank into herself, and drew back.

'An enemy? What enemy?' asked Mrs Lodge.

He shook his head. 'That's best known to yourself,' he said. 'If you like, I can show the person to you, though I shall not myself know who it is. I can do no more; and don't wish to do that.'

She pressed him; on which he told Rhoda to wait outside where she stood, and took Mrs Lodge into the room. It opened immediately from the door; and, as the latter remained ajar, Rhoda Brook could see the proceedings without taking part in them. He brought a tumbler from the dresser, nearly filled it with water, and fetching an egg, prepared it in some private way; after which he broke it on the edge of the glass, so that the white went in and the yolk remained. As it was getting gloomy, he took the glass and its contents to the window, and told Gertrude to watch the mixture closely. They leant over the table together, and the milkwoman could see the opaline hue of the egg-fluid changing form as it sank in the water, but she was not near enough to define the shape that it assumed.

'Do you catch the likeness of any face or figure as you look?' demanded the conjuror of the young woman.

She murmured a reply, in tones so low as to be inaudible to Rhoda, and continued to gaze intently into the glass. Rhoda turned, and walked a few steps away.

When Mrs Lodge came out, and her face was met by the light, it appeared exceedingly pale—as pale as Rhoda's—against the sad dun shades of the upland's garniture. Trendle shut the door behind her, and they at once started homeward together. But Rhoda perceived that her companion had quite changed.

'Did he charge much?' she asked tentatively.

'O no—nothing, He would not take a farthing,' said Gertrude.

'And what did you see?' inquired Rhoda.

'Nothing I—care to speak of.' The constraint in her manner was remarkable; her face was so rigid as to wear an oldened aspect, faintly suggestive of the face in Rhoda's bedchamber.

'Was it you who first proposed coming here?' Mrs Lodge suddenly inquired, after a long pause. 'How very odd, if you did!'

'No. But I am not very sorry we have come, all things considered.' she replied. For the first time a sense of triumph possessed her, and she did not altogether deplore that the young thing at her side should learn that their lives had been antagonized by other influences than their own.

The subject was no more alluded to during the long and dreary walk home. But in some way or other a story was whispered about the many-dairied lowland that winter that Mrs Lodge's gradual loss of the use of her left arm was owing to her being 'overlooked' by Rhoda Brook. The latter kept her own counsel about the incubus, but her face grew sadder and thinner; and in the spring she and her boy disappeared from the neighbourhood of Holmstoke.

VI
A Second Attempt

Half a dozen years passed away, and Mr and Mrs Lodge's married experience sank into prosiness, and worse. The farmer was usually gloomy and silent: the woman whom he had wooed for her grace and beauty was contorted and disfigured in the left limb; moreover, she had brought him no child, which rendered it likely that he would be the last of a family who had occupied that valley for some two hundred years. He thought of Rhoda Brook and her son; and feared this might be a judgement from heaven upon him.

The once blithe-hearted and enlightened Gertrude was changing into an irritable, superstitious woman, whose whole time was given to experimenting upon her ailment with every quack remedy she came across. She was honestly attached to her husband, and was ever secretly hoping against hope to win back his heart again by regaining some at least of her personal beauty. Hence it arose that her closet was lined with bottles, packets, and ointment-pots of every description—nay, bunches of mystic herbs, charms, and books of necromancy, which in her schoolgirl time she would have ridiculed as folly.

'Damned if you won't poison yourself with these apothecary messes and witch mixtures some time or other,' said her husband, when his eye chanced to fall upon the multitudinous array.

She did not reply, but turned her sad, soft glance upon him in such heart-swollen reproach that he looked sorry for his words, and added, 'I only meant it for your good, you know, Gertrude.'

'I'll clear out the whole lot, and destroy them,' said she huskily, 'and try such remedies no more!'

'You want somebody to cheer you,' he observed. 'I once thought of adopting a boy; but he is too old now. And he is gone away I don't know where.'

She guessed to whom he alluded; for Rhoda Brook's story had in the course of years become known to her; though not a word had ever passed between her husband and herself on the subject. Neither had she ever spoken to him of her visit to Conjuror Trendle, and of what was revealed to her, or she thought was revealed to her, by that solitary heath-man.

She was now five-and-twenty; but she seemed older. 'Six years of marriage, and only a few months of love,' she sometimes whispered to herself. And then she thought of the apparent cause, and said, with a tragic glance at her withering limb, 'If I could only be again as I was when he first saw me!'

She obediently destroyed her nostrums and charms; but there remained a hankering wish to try something else—some other sort of cure altogether. She had never revisited Trendle since she had been conducted to the house of the solitary by Rhoda against her will; but it now suddenly occurred to Gertrude that she would, in a last desperate effort at deliverance from this seeming curse, again seek out the man, if he yet lived. He was entitled to a certain credence, for the indistinct form he had raised in the glass had undoubtedly resembled the only woman in the world who—as she now knew, though not then—could have a reason for bearing her ill-will. The visit should be paid.

This time she went alone, though she nearly got lost on the heath, and roamed a considerable distance out of her way. Trendle's house was reached at last; however, he was not indoors, and instead of waiting at the cottage, she went to where his bent figure was pointed out to her at work a long way off. Trendle remembered her, and laying down the handful of furze-roots which he was gathering and throwing into a heap, he offered to accompany her in her homeward direction, as the distance was considerable and the days were short. So they walked together, his head bowed nearly to the earth, and his form of a colour with it.

'You can send away warts and other excrescences, I know,' she said; 'why can't you send away this?' And the arm was uncovered.

'You think too much of my powers!' said Trendle; 'and I

am old and weak now, too. No, no; it is too much for me to attempt in my own person. What have ye tried?'

She named to him some of the hundred medicaments and counterspells which she had adopted from time to time. He shook his head.

'Some were good enough,' he said approvingly; 'but not many of them for such as this. This is of the nature of a blight, not of the nature of a wound; and if you ever do throw it off, it will be all at once.'

'If I only could!'

'There is only one chance of doing it known to me. It has never failed in kindred afflictions—that I can declare. But it is hard to carry out, and especially for a woman.'

'Tell me!' said she.

'You must touch with the limb the neck of a man who's been hanged.'

She started a little at the image he had raised.

'Before he's cold—just after he's cut down,' continued the conjuror impassively.

'How can that do good?'

'It will turn the blood and change the constitution. But, as I say, to do it is hard. You must get into jail, and wait for him when he's brought off the gallows. Lots have done it, though perhaps not such pretty women as you. I used to send dozens for skin complaints. But that was in former times. The last I sent was in '13—near twenty years ago.'

He had no more to tell her; and, when he had put her into a straight track homeward, turned and left her, refusing all money as at first.

VII
A Ride

The communication sank deep into Gertrude's mind. Her nature was rather a timid one; and probably of all remedies that the white wizard could have suggested there was not one which would have filled her with so much aversion as this, not to speak of the immense obstacles in the way of its adoption.

Casterbridge, the county-town, was a dozen or fifteen miles off; and though in those days, when men were executed for horse-stealing, arson, and burglary, an assize seldom passed without a hanging, it was not likely that she could get access to the body of the criminal unaided. And the fear of her husband's anger made her reluctant to breathe a word of Trendle's suggestion to him or to anybody about him.

She did nothing for months, and patiently bore her disfigurement as before. But her woman's nature, craving for renewed love, through the medium of renewed beauty (she was but twenty-five), was ever stimulating her to try what, at any rate, could hardly do her any harm. 'What came by a spell will go by a spell surely,' she would say. Whenever her imagination pictured the act she shrank in terror from the possibility of it: then the words of the conjuror, 'It will turn your blood', were seen to be capable of a scientific no less than ghastly interpretation; the mastering desire returned, and urged her on again.

There was at this time but one county paper, and that her husband only occasionally borrowed. But old-fashioned days had old-fashioned means, and news was extensively conveyed by word of mouth from market to market, or from fair to fair, so that, whenever such an event as an execution was about to take place, few within a radius of twenty miles were ignorant of the coming sight; and, so far as Holmstoke was concerned, some enthusiasts had been known to walk all the way to Casterbridge and back in one day, solely to witness the spectacle. The next assizes were in March; and when Gertrude Lodge heard that they had been held, she inquired stealthily at the inn as to the result, as soon as she could find opportunity.

She was, however, too late. The time at which the sentences were to be carried out had arrived, and to make the journey and obtain permission at such short notice required at least her husband's assistance. She dared not tell him, for she had found by delicate experiment that these smouldering village beliefs made him furious if mentioned, partly because he half entertained them himself. It was therefore necessary to wait for another opportunity.

Her determination received a fillip from learning that two epileptic children had attended from this very village of Holmstoke many years before with beneficial results, though the experiment had been strongly condemned by the neighbouring clergy. April, May, June, passed; and it is no overstatement to say that by the end of the last-named month Gertrude well-nigh longed for the death of a fellow-creature. Instead of her formal prayers each night, her unconscious prayer was, 'O Lord, hang some guilty or innocent person soon!'

This time she made earlier inquiries, and was altogether more systematic in her proceedings. Moreover, the season was summer, between the haymaking and the harvest, and in the leisure thus afforded him her husband had been holiday-taking away from home.

The assizes were in July, and she went to the inn as before. There was to be one execution—only one—for arson.

Her greatest problem was not how to get to Casterbridge, but what means she should adopt for obtaining admission to the jail. Though access for such purposes had formerly never been denied, the custom had fallen into desuetude; and in contemplating her possible difficulties, she was again almost driven to fall back upon her husband. But, on sounding him about the assizes, he was so uncommunicative, so more than usually cold, that she did not proceed, and decided that whatever she did she would do alone.

Fortune, obdurate hitherto, showed her unexpected favour. On the Thursday before the Saturday fixed for the execution, Lodge remarked to her that he was going away from home for another day or two on business at a fair, and that he was sorry he could not take her with him.

She exhibited on this occasion so much readiness to stay at home that he looked at her in surprise. Time had been when she would have shown deep disappointment at the loss of such a jaunt. However, he lapsed into his usual taciturnity, and on the day named left Holmstoke.

It was now her turn. She at first had thought of driving, but on reflection held that driving would not do, since it would necessitate her keeping to the turnpike road, and so increase by tenfold the risk of her ghastly errand being found out. She decided to ride, and avoid the beaten track, notwithstanding that in her husband's stables there was no animal just at present which by any stretch of imagination could be considered a lady's mount, in spite of his promise before marriage to always keep a mare for her. He had, however, many cart-horses, fine ones of their kind; and among the rest was a serviceable creature, an equine Amazon, with a back as broad as a sofa, on which Gertrude had occasionally taken an airing when unwell. This horse she chose.

On Friday afternoon one of the men brought it round. She was dressed, and before going down looked at her shrivelled arm. 'Ah!' she said to it, 'if it had not been for you this terrible ordeal would have been saved me!'

When strapping up the bundle in which she carried a few articles of clothing, she took occasion to say to the servant, 'I take these in case I should not get back tonight from the person I am going to visit. Don't be alarmed if I am not in by ten, and close up the house as usual. I shall be home tomorrow for certain.' She meant then to privately tell her husband: the deed accomplished was not like the deed projected. He would almost certainly forgive her.

And then the pretty palpitating Gertrude Lodge went from her husband's homestead; but though her goal was Casterbridge she did not take the direct route thither through Stickleford. Her cunning course at first was in precisely the opposite direction. As soon as she was out of sight, however, she turned to the left, by a road which led into Egdon, and on entering the heath wheeled round, and set out in the true course, due westerly. A more private way down the county could not be imagined; and as to direction, she had merely to keep her horse's head to a point a little to the right of the sun. She knew that she would light upon a furze-cutter or cottager of some sort from time to time, from whom she might correct her bearing.

Though the date was comparatively recent, Egdon was much less fragmentary in character than now. The attempts—successful and otherwise—at cultivation on the lower slopes, which intrude and break up the original heath into small detached heaths, had not been carried far; Enclosure Acts had not taken effect, and the banks and fences which now exclude the cattle of those villagers who formerly enjoyed rights of commonage thereon, and the carts of those who had turbary privileges which kept them in firing all the year round, were not erected. Gertrude, therefore, rode along with no other obstacles than the prickly furze-bushes, the mats of heather, the white water-courses, and the natural steeps and declivities of the ground.

Her horse was sure, if heavy-footed and slow, and though a draught animal, was easy-paced; had it been otherwise, she was not a woman who could have ventured to ride over such a bit of country with a half-dead arm. It was therefore nearly eight o'clock when she drew rein to breathe the mare on the last outlying high point of heathland towards Casterbridge, previous to leaving Egdon for the cultivated valleys.

She halted before a pool called Rushy-pond, flanked by the ends of two hedges; a railing ran through the centre of the pond, dividing it in half. Over the railing she saw the low green country; over the green trees the roofs of the town; over the roofs a white flat façade, denoting the entrance to the county jail. On the roof of this front specks were moving about; they seemed to be workmen erecting something. Her flesh crept. She descended slowly, and was soon amid cornfields and pastures. In another half-hour, when it was almost dusk, Gertrude reached the White Hart, the first inn of the town on that side.

Little surprise was excited by her arrival; farmers' wives rode on horseback then more than they do now; though, for that matter, Mrs Lodge was not imagined to be a wife at all; the innkeeper supposed her some harum-scarum young woman who had come to attend 'hang-fair' next day. Neither her husband nor herself ever dealt in Casterbridge market, so that she was unknown. While dismounting she beheld a crowd of boys standing at the door of a harness-maker's shop just above the inn, looking inside it with deep interest.

'What is going on there?' she asked of the ostler.

'Making the rope for tomorrow.'

She throbbed responsively, and contracted her arm.

"Tis sold by the inch afterwards,' the man continued. 'I could get you a bit, miss, for nothing, if you'd like?'

She hastily repudiated any such wish, all the more from a curious creeping feeling that the condemned wretch's destiny was becoming interwoven with her own; and having engaged a room for the night, sat down to think.

Up to this time she had formed but the vaguest notions

about her means of obtaining access to the prison. The words of the cunning-man returned to her mind. He had implied that she should use her beauty, impaired though it was, as a pass-key. In her inexperience she knew little about jail functionaries; she had heard of a high-sheriff and an under-sheriff; but dimly only. She knew, however, that there must be a hangman, and to the hangman she determined to apply.

VIII
A Waterside Hermit

At this date, and for several years after, there was a hangman to almost every jail. Gertrude found, on inquiry, that the Casterbridge official dwelt in a lonely cottage by a deep slow river flowing under the cliff on which the prison buildings were situate—the stream being the self-same one, though she did not know it, which watered the Stickleford and Holmstoke meads lower down in its course.

Having changed her dress, and before she had eaten or drunk—for she could not take her ease till she had ascertained some particulars—Gertrude pursued her way by a path along the waterside to the cottage indicated. Passing thus the outskirts of the jail, she discerned on the level roof over the gateway three rectangular lines against the sky, where the specks had been moving in her distant view; she recognized what the erection was, and passed quickly on, Another hundred yards brought her to the executioner's house, which a boy pointed out. It stood close to the same stream, and was hard by a weir, the waters of which emitted a steady roar.

While she stood hesitating the door opened, and an old man came forth shading a candle with one hand. Locking the door on the outside, he turned to a flight of wooden steps fixed against the end of the cottage, and began to ascend them, this being evidently the staircase to his bedroom. Gertrude hastened forward, but by the time she reached the foot of the ladder he was at the top. She called to him loudly enough to be heard above the roar of the weir; he looked down and said, 'What d'ye want here?'

'To speak to you a minute.'

The candlelight, such as it was, fell upon her imploring, pale, upturned face, and Davies (as the hangman was called) backed down the ladder. 'I was just going to bed,' he said; '"Early to bed and early to rise", but I don't mind stopping a minute for such a one as you. Come into house.' He reopened the door, and preceded her to the room within.

The implements of his daily work, which was that of a jobbing gardener, stood in a corner, and seeing probably that she looked rural, he said, 'If you want me to undertake country work I can't come, for I never leave Casterbridge for gentle nor simple—not I. My real calling is officer of justice,' he added formally.

'Yes, yes! That's it. Tomorrow!'

'Ah! I thought so. Well, what's the matter about that? 'Tis no use to come here about the knot—folks do come continually, but I tell 'em one knot is as merciful as another if ye keep it under the ear. Is the unfortunate man a relation; or, I should say, perhaps,' (looking at her dress) 'a person who's been in your employ?'

'No. What time is the execution?'

'The same as usual—twelve o'clock, or as soon after as the London mail-coach gets in. We always wait for that, in case of a reprieve.'

'O—a reprieve—I hope not!' she said involuntarily.

'Well,—hee, hee!—as a matter of business, so do I! But still, if ever a young fellow deserved to be let off, this one does; only just turned eighteen, and only present by chance when the rick was fired. Howsomever, there's not much risk of that, as they are obliged to make an example of him, there having been so much destruction of property that way lately.'

'I mean,' she explained, 'that I want to touch him for a charm, a cure of an affliction, by the advice of a man who has proved the virtue of the remedy.'

'O yes, miss! Now I understand. I've had such people come in past years. But it didn't strike me that you looked of a sort to require blood-turning. What's the complaint? The wrong kind for this, I'll be bound.'

'My arm.' She reluctantly showed the withered skin.

'Ah!—'tis all a-scram!' said the hangman, examining it.

'Yes,' said she.

'Well,' he continued, with interest, 'that *is* the class o' subject, I'm bound to admit! I like the look of the place; it is truly as suitable for the cure as any I ever saw. 'Twas a knowing man that sent 'ee, whoever he was.'

'You can contrive for me all that's necessary?' she said breathlessly.

'You should really have gone to the governor of the jail, and your doctor with 'ee, and given your name and address—that's how it used to be done, if I recollect. Still, perhaps, I can manage it for a trifling fee.'

'O, thank you! I would rather do it this way, as I should like it kept private.'

'Lover not to know, eh?'

'No—husband.'

'Aha! Very well. I'll get 'ee a touch of the corpse.'

'Where is it now?' she said, shuddering.

'It?—*he*, you mean; he's living yet. Just inside that little small winder up there in the glum.' He signified the jail on the cliff above.

She thought of her husband and her friends. 'Yes, of course,' she said; 'and how am I to proceed?'

He took her to the door. 'Now, do you be waiting at the little wicket in the wall, that you'll find up there in the lane, not later than one o'clock. I will open it from the inside, as I shan't come home to dinner till he's cut down. Good-night. Be punctual; and if you don't want anybody to know 'ee, wear a veil. Ah—once I had such a daughter as you!'

She went away, and climbed the path above, to assure herself that she would be able to find the wicket next day. Its outline was soon visible to her—a narrow opening in the outer wall of the prison precincts. The steep was so great that, having reached the wicket, she stopped a moment to breathe; and, looking back upon the waterside cot, saw the hangman again ascending his outdoor staircase.' He entered the loft or chamber to which it led, and in a few minutes extinguished his light.

The town clock struck ten, and she returned to the White Hart as she had come.

IX
A Rencounter

It was one o'clock on Saturday. Gertrude Lodge, having been admitted to the jail as above described, was sitting in a waiting-room within the second gate, which stood under a classic archway of ashlar, then comparatively modern, and bearing the inscription, 'Covnty Jail: 1793.' This had been the façade she saw from the heath the day before. Near at hand was a passage to the roof on which the gallows stood.

The town was thronged, and the market suspended; but Gertrude had seen scarcely a soul. Having kept her room till the hour of the appointment, she had proceeded to the spot by a way which avoided the open space below the cliff where the spectators had gathered; but she could, even now, hear the multitudinous babble of their voices, out of which rose at intervals the hoarse croak of a single voice uttering the words, 'Last dying speech and confession!' There had been no reprieve, and the execution was over; but the crowd still waited to see the body taken down.

Soon the persistent woman heard a trampling overhead, then a hand beckoned to her, and, following directions, she went out and crossed the inner paved court beyond the gatehouse, her knees trembling so that she could scarcely walk. One of her arms was out of its sleeve, and only covered by her shawl.

On the spot at which she had now arrived were two trestles, and before she could think of their purpose she heard heavy feet descending stairs somewhere at her back. Turn her head she would not, or could not, and, rigid in this position, she was conscious of a rough coffin passing her shoulder, borne by four men. It was open, and in it lay the body of a young man, wearing the smock-frock of a rustic, and fustian breeches. The corpse had been thrown into the coffin so hastily that the skirt of the smock-frock was hanging over. The burden was temporarily deposited on the trestles.

By this time the young woman's state was such that a grey mist seemed to float before her eyes, on account of which, and the veil she wore, she could scarcely discern anything: it was as though she had nearly died, but was held up by a sort of galvanism.

'Now!' said a voice close at hand, and she was just conscious that the word had been addressed to her.

By a last strenuous effort she advanced, at the same time hearing persons approaching behind her. She bared her poor curst arm; and Davies, uncovering the face of the corpse, took Gertrude's hand, and held it so that her arm lay across the dead man's neck, upon a line the colour of an unripe blackberry, which surrounded it.

Gertrude shrieked: 'the turn o' the blood', predicted by the conjuror, had taken place. But at that moment a second shriek rent the air of the enclosure: it was not Gertrude's, and its effect upon her was to make her start round.

Immediately behind her stood Rhoda Brook, her face drawn, and her eyes red with weeping. Behind Rhoda stood Gertrude's own husband; his countenance lined, his eyes dim, but without a tear.

'Damn you! What are you doing here?' he said hoarsely.

'Hussy—to come between us and our child now!' cried Rhoda. 'This is the meaning of what Satan showed me in the vision! You are like her at last!' And clutching the bare arm of the younger woman, she pulled her unresistingly back against the wall. Immediately Rhoda had loosened her hold the fragile young Gertrude slid down against the feet of her husband. When he lifted her up she was unconscious.

The mere sight of the twain had been enough to suggest to her that the dead young man was Rhoda's son. At that time the relatives of an executed convict had the privilege of claiming the body for burial, if they chose to do so; and it was for this purpose that Lodge was awaiting the inquest with Rhoda. He had been summoned by her as soon as the young man was taken in the crime, and at different times since; and he had attended in court during the trial. This was the 'holiday' he had been indulging in of late. The two wretched parents had wished to avoid exposure; and hence had come themselves for the body, a wagon and sheet for its conveyance and covering being in waiting outside.

Gertrude's case was so serious that it was deemed advisable to call to her the surgeon who was at hand. She was taken out of the jail into the town; but she never reached home alive. Her delicate vitality, sapped perhaps by the paralyzed arm, collapsed under the double shock that followed the severe strain, physical and mental, to which she had subjected herself during the previous twenty-four hours. Her blood had been 'turned' indeed—too far. Her death took place in the town three days after.

Her husband was never seen in Casterbridge again; once only in the old marketplace at Anglebury, which he had so much frequented, and very seldom in public anywhere. Burdened at first with moodiness and remorse, he eventually changed for the better, and appeared as a chastened and thoughtful man. Soon after attending the funeral of his poor young wife he took steps towards giving up the farms in Holmstoke and the adjoining parish, and, having sold every head of his stock, he went away to Port-Bredy, at the other end of the county, living there in solitary lodgings till his death two years later of a painless decline. It was then found that he had bequeathed the whole of his not inconsiderable property to a reformatory for boys, subject to the payment of a small annuity to Rhoda Brook, if she could be found to claim it.

For some time she could not be found; but eventually she reappeared in her old parish,—absolutely refusing, however, to have anything to do with the provision made for her. Her monotonous milking at the dairy was resumed, and followed for many long years, till her form became bent, and her once abundant dark hair white and worn away at the forehead— perhaps by long pressure against the cows. Here, sometimes, those who knew her experiences would stand and observe her, and wonder what sombre thoughts were beating inside that impassive, wrinkled brow, to the rhythm of the alternating milk-streams.

3

THE THREE STRANGERS

Among the few features of agricultural England which retain an appearance but little modified by the lapse of centuries, may be reckoned the high, grassy and furzy downs, coombs, or ewe-leases, as they are indifferently called, that fill a large area of certain counties in the south and southwest. If any mark of human occupation is met with hereon, it usually takes the form of the solitary cottage of some shepherd.

Fifty years ago such a lonely cottage stood on such a down, and may possibly be standing there now. In spite of its loneliness, however, the spot, by actual measurement, was not more than five miles from a county-town. Yet that affected it little. Five miles of irregular upland, during the long inimical seasons, with their sleets, snows, rains, and mists, afford withdrawing space enough to isolate a Timon or a Nebuchadnezzar; much less, in fair weather, to please that less repellent tribe, the poets, philosophers, artists, and others who 'conceive and meditate of pleasant things'.

Some old earthen camp or barrow, some clump of trees, at least some starved fragment of ancient hedge is usually taken advantage of in the erection of these forlorn dwellings. But, in the present case, such a kind of shelter had been disregarded. Higher Crowstairs, as the house was called, stood quite detached and undefended. The only reason for its precise situation seemed to be the crossing of two footpaths at right angles hard by, which may have crossed there and thus for a good five hundred years. Hence the house was exposed to the elements on all sides. But, though the wind up here blew unmistakably when it did blow, and the rain hit hard whenever it fell, the various weathers of the winter season were not quite so formidable on the coomb as they were imagined to be by dwellers on low ground. The raw rimes were not so pernicious as in the hollows, and the frosts were scarcely so severe. When the shepherd and his family who tenanted the house were pitied for their sufferings from the exposure, they said that upon the whole they were less inconvenienced by 'wuzzes and flames' (hoarses and phlegms) than when they had lived by the stream of a snug neighbouring valley.

The night of 28 March, 182—, was precisely one of the nights that were wont to call forth these expressions of commiseration. The level rainstorm smote walls, slopes, and hedges like the clothyard shafts of Senlac and Crecy. Such sheep and outdoor animals as had no shelter stood with their buttocks to the winds; while the tails of little birds trying to roost on some scraggy thorn were blown inside-out like umbrellas. The gable-end of the cottage was stained with wet, and the eavesdroppings flapped against the wall. Yet never was commiseration for the shepherd more misplaced. For that cheerful rustic was entertaining a large party in glorification of the christening of his second girl.

The guests had arrived before the rain began to fall, and they were all now assembled in the chief or living-room of the dwelling. A glance into the apartment at eight o'clock on this eventful evening would have resulted in the opinion that it was as cosy and comfortable a nook as could be wished for in boisterous weather. The calling of its inhabitant was proclaimed by a number of highly-polished sheep-crooks without stems that were hung ornamentally over the fireplace, the curl of each shining crook varying from the antiquated type engraved in the patriarchal pictures of old family Bibles to the most approved fashion of the last local sheep-fair. The room was lighted by half-a-dozen candles, having wicks only a trifle smaller than the grease which enveloped them, in candlesticks that were never used but at high-days, holy-days, and family feasts. The lights were scattered about the room, two of them standing on the chimney-piece. This position of candles was in itself significant. Candles on the chimney-piece always meant a party.

On the hearth, in front of a back-brand to give substance, blazed a fire of thorns, that crackled 'like the laughter of the fool'.

Nineteen persons were gathered here. Of these, five women, wearing gowns of various bright hues, sat in chairs along the wall; girls shy and not shy filled the window-bench; four men, including Charley Jake the hedge-carpenter, Elijah New the parish-clerk, and John Pitcher, a neighbouring dairyman, the shepherd's father-in-law, lolled in the settle; a young man and maid, who were blushing over tentative pourparlers on a life-companionship, sat beneath the corner-cupboard; and an elderly engaged man of fifty or upward moved restlessly about from spots where his betrothed was not to the spot where she was. Enjoyment was pretty general, and so much the more prevailed in being unhampered by conventional restrictions. Absolute confidence in each other's good opinion begat perfect ease, while the finishing stroke of manner, amounting to a truly princely serenity, was lent to the majority by the absence of any expression or trait denoting that they wished to get on in the world, enlarge their minds, or do any eclipsing thing whatever—which nowadays so generally nips the bloom and bonhomie of all except the two extremes of the social scale.

Shepherd Fennel had married well, his wife being a dairyman's daughter from a vale at a distance, who brought fifty guineas in her pocket—and kept them there, till they should be required for ministering to the needs of a coming family. This frugal woman had been somewhat exercised as to the character that should be given to the gathering. A sit-still party had its advantages; but an undisturbed position of ease in chairs and settles was apt to lead on the men to such an unconscionable deal of toping that they would sometimes fairly drink the house dry. A dancing-party was the alternative; but this, while avoiding the foregoing objection on the score of good drink, had a counterbalancing disadvantage in the matter of good victuals, the ravenous appetites engendered by the exercise causing immense havoc in the buttery. Shepherdess Fennel fell back upon the intermediate plan of mingling short dances with short periods of talk and singing, so as to hinder any ungovernable rage in either. But this scheme was entirely confined to her own gentle mind: the shepherd himself was in the mood to exhibit the most reckless phases of hospitality.

The fiddler was a boy of those parts, about twelve years of age, who had a wonderful dexterity in jigs and reels, though his fingers were so small and short as to necessitate a constant shifting for the high notes, from which he scrambled back to the first position with sounds not of unmixed purity of tone. At seven the shrill tweedle-dee of this youngster had begun, accompanied by a booming ground-bass from Elijah New, the parish-clerk, who had thoughtfully brought with him his favourite musical instrument, the serpent. Dancing was instantaneous, Mrs Fennel privately enjoining the players on no account to let the dance exceed the length of a quarter of an hour.

But Elijah and the boy, in the excitement of their position, quite forgot the injunction. Moreover, Oliver Giles, a man of seventeen, one of the dancers, who was enamoured of his partner, a fair girl of thirty-three rolling years, had recklessly handed a new crown-piece to the musicians, as a bribe to keep going as long as they had muscle and wind. Mrs Fennel, seeing the steam begin to generate on the countenances of her guests, crossed over and touched the fiddler's elbow and put her hand on the serpent's mouth. But they took no notice, and fearing she might lose her character of genial hostess if she were to interfere too markedly, she retired and sat down helpless. And so the dance whizzed on with cumulative fury, the performers moving in their planet-like courses, direct and retrograde, from apogee to perigee, till the hand of the well-kicked clock at the bottom of the room had travelled over the circumference of an hour.

While these cheerful events were in course of enactment within Fennel's pastoral dwelling, an incident having considerable bearing on the party had occurred in the gloomy night without. Mrs Fennel's concern about the growing fierceness of the dance corresponded in point of time with the ascent of a human figure to the solitary hill of Higher Crowstairs from the direction of the distant town. This personage strode on through the rain without a pause, following the little-worn path which, further on in its course, skirted the shepherd's cottage.

It was nearly the time of full moon, and on this account, though the sky was lined with a uniform sheet of dripping cloud, ordinary objects out of doors were readily visible. The sad wan light revealed the lonely pedestrian to be a man of supple frame; his gait suggested that he had somewhat passed the period of perfect and instinctive agility, though not so far as to be otherwise than rapid of motion when occasion required. At a rough guess, he might have been about forty years of age. He appeared tall, but a recruiting sergeant, or other person accustomed to the judging of men's heights by the eye, would have discerned that this was chiefly owing to his gauntness, and that he was not more than five-feet-eight or nine.

Notwithstanding the regularity of his tread, there was caution in it, as in that of one who mentally feels his way; and despite the fact that it was not a black coat nor a dark garment of any sort that he wore, there was something about him which suggested that he naturally belonged to the black-coated tribes of men. His clothes were of fustian, and his boots hobnailed, yet in his progress he showed not the mud-accustomed bearing of hobnailed and fustianed peasantry.

By the time that he had arrived abreast of the shepherd's premises the rain came down, or rather came along, with yet more determined violence. The outskirts of the little settlement partially broke the force of wind and rain, and this induced him to stand still. The most salient of the shepherd's domestic erections was an empty sty at the forward corner of his hedgeless garden, for in these latitudes the principle of masking the homelier features of your establishment by a conventional frontage was unknown. The traveller's eye was attracted to this small building by the pallid shine of the wet slates that covered it. He turned aside, and, finding it empty, stood under the pent-roof for shelter.

While he stood, the boom of the serpent within the adjacent house, and the lesser strains of the fiddler, reached the spot as an accompaniment to the surging hiss of the flying rain on the sod, its louder beating on the cabbage-leaves of the garden, on the eight or ten beehives just discernible by the path, and its dripping from the eaves into a row of buckets and pans that had been placed under the walls of the cottage. For at Higher Crowstairs, as at all such elevated domiciles, the grand difficulty of housekeeping was an insufficiency of water; and a casual rainfall was utilized by turning out, as catchers, every utensil that the house contained. Some queer stories might be told of the contrivances for economy in suds and dishwaters that are absolutely necessitated in upland habitations during the droughts of summer. But at this season there were no such exigencies; a mere acceptance of what the skies bestowed was sufficient for an abundant store.

At last the notes of the serpent ceased and the house was silent. This cessation of activity aroused the solitary pedestrian from the reverie into which he had lapsed, and, emerging from the shed, with an apparently new intention, he walked up the path to the house-door. Arrived here, his first act was to kneel down on a large stone beside the row of vessels, and to drink a copious draught from one of them. Having quenched his thirst he rose and lifted his hand to knock, but paused with his eye upon the panel. Since the dark surface of the wood revealed absolutely nothing, it was evident that he must be mentally looking through the door, as if he wished to measure thereby all the possibilities that a house of this sort might include, and how they might bear upon the question of his entry.

In his indecision he turned and surveyed the scene around. Not a soul was anywhere visible. The garden-path stretched downward from his feet, gleaming like the track of a snail; the roof of the little well (mostly dry), the well-cover, the top rail of the garden-gate, were varnished with the same dull liquid glaze; while, far away in the vale, a faint whiteness of more than usual extent showed that the rivers were high in the meads. Beyond all this winked a few bleared lamplights through the beating drops—lights that denoted the situation of the county-town from which he had appeared to come. The absence of all notes of life in that direction seemed to clinch his intentions, and he knocked at the door.

Within, a desultory chat had taken the place of movement and musical sound. The hedge-carpenter was suggesting a song to the company, which nobody just then was inclined to undertake, so that the knock afforded a not unwelcome diversion.

'Walk in!' said the shepherd promptly.

The latch clicked upward, and out of the night our pedestrian appeared upon the doormat. The shepherd arose, snuffed two of the nearest candles, and turned to look at him.

Their light disclosed that the stranger was dark in complexion and not unprepossessing as to feature. His hat, which for a moment he did not remove, hung low over his eyes, without concealing that they were large, open, and determined, moving with a flash rather than a glance round the room. He seemed pleased with his survey, and, baring his shaggy head, said, in a rich deep voice, 'The rain is so heavy, friends, that I ask leave to come in and rest awhile.'

'To be sure, stranger,' said the shepherd. 'And faith, you've been lucky in choosing your time, for we are having a bit of a fling for a glad cause—though, to be sure, a man could hardly wish that glad cause to happen more than once a year.'

'Nor less,' spoke up a woman. 'For 'tis best to get your family over and done with, as soon as you can, so as to be all the earlier out of the fag o't.'

'And what may be this glad cause?' asked the stranger.

'A birth and christening,' said the shepherd.

The stranger hoped his host might not be made unhappy either by too many or too few of such episodes, and being invited by a gesture to a pull at the mug, he readily acquiesced. His manner, which, before entering, had been so dubious, was now altogether that of a careless and candid man.

'Late to be traipsing athwart this coomb—hey?' said the engaged man of fifty.

'Late it is, master, as you say.—I'll take a seat in the chimney-corner, if you have nothing to urge against it, ma'am; for I am a little moist on the side that was next the rain.'

Mrs Shepherd Fennel assented, and made room for the self-invited comer, who, having got completely inside the chimney-corner, stretched out his legs and his arms with the expansiveness of a person quite at home.

'Yes, I am rather cracked in the vamp,' he said freely, seeing that the eyes of the shepherd's wife fell upon his boots, 'and I am not well fitted either. I have had some rough times lately, and have been forced to pick up what I can get in the way of wearing, but I must find a suit better fit for working-days when I reach home.'

'One of hereabouts?' she inquired.

'Not quite that—further up the country.'

'I thought so. And so be I; and by your tongue you come from my neighbourhood.'

'But you would hardly have heard of me,' he said quickly. 'My time would be long before yours, ma'am, you see.'

This testimony to the youthfulness of his hostess had the effect of stopping her cross-examination.

'There is only one thing more wanted to make me happy,' continued the newcomer. 'And that is a little baccy, which I am sorry to say I am out of.'

'I'll fill your pipe,' said the shepherd.

'I must ask you to lend me a pipe likewise.'

'A smoker, and no pipe about 'ee?'

'I have dropped it somewhere on the road.'

The shepherd filled and handed him a new clay pipe, saying, as he did so, 'Hand me your baccy-box—I'll fill that too, now I am about it.'

The man went through the movement of searching his pockets.

'Lost that too?' said his entertainer, with some surprise.

'I am afraid so,' said the man with some confusion. 'Give it to me in a screw of paper.' Lighting his pipe at the candle with a suction that drew the whole flame into the bowl, he resettled himself in the corner and bent his looks upon the faint steam from his damp legs, as if he wished to say no more.

Meanwhile the general body of guests had been taking little notice of this visitor by reason of an absorbing discussion in which they were engaged with the band about a tune for the next dance. The matter being settled, they were about to stand up when an interruption came in the shape of another knock at the door.

At sound of the same the man in the chimney-corner took up the poker and began stirring the brands as if doing it thoroughly were the one aim of his existence; and a second time the shepherd said, 'Walk in!' In a moment another man stood upon the straw-woven doormat. He too was a stranger.

This individual was one of a type radically different from the first. There was more of the commonplace in his manner, and a certain jovial cosmopolitanism sat upon his features. He was several years older than the first arrival, his hair being slightly frosted, his eyebrows bristly, and his whiskers cut back from his cheeks. His face was rather full and flabby, and yet it was not altogether a face without power. A few grog-blossoms marked the neighbourhood of his nose. He flung back his long drab greatcoat, revealing that beneath it he wore a suit of cinder-grey shade throughout, large heavy seals, of some metal or other that would take a polish, dangling from his fob as his only personal ornament. Shaking the water-drops from his low-crowned glazed hat, he said, 'I must ask for a few minutes' shelter, comrades, or I shall be wetted to my skin before I get to Casterbridge.'

'Make yourself at home, master,' said the shepherd, perhaps a trifle less heartily than on the first occasion. Not that Fennel had the least tinge of niggardliness in his composition; but the room was far from large, spare chairs were not numerous, and damp companions were not altogether desirable at close quarters for the women and girls in their bright-coloured gowns.

However, the second comer, after taking off his greatcoat, and hanging his hat on a nail in one of the ceiling-beams as if he had been specially invited to put it there, advanced and sat down at the table. This had been pushed so closely into the chimney-corner, to give all available room to the dancers, that its inner edge grazed the elbow of the man who had ensconced himself by the fire; and thus the two strangers were brought into close companionship. They nodded to each other by way of breaking the ice of unacquaintance, and the first stranger handed his neighbour the family mug—a huge vessel of brown ware, having its upper edge worn away like a threshold by the rub of whole generations of thirsty lips that had gone the way of all flesh, and bearing the following inscription burnt upon its rotund side in yellow letters:

THERE IS NO FUN
UNTILL I CUM.

The other man, nothing loth, raised the mug to his lips, and drank on, and on, and on—till a curious blueness overspread the countenance of the shepherd's wife, who had regarded with no little surprise the first stranger's free offer to the second of what did not belong to him to dispense.

'I knew it!' said the toper to the shepherd with much satisfaction. 'When I walked up your garden before coming in, and saw the hives all of a row, I said to myself; "Where there's bees there's honey, and where there's honey there's mead." But mead of such a truly comfortable sort as this I really didn't expect to meet in my older days.' He took yet another pull at the mug, till it assumed an ominous elevation.

'Glad you enjoy it!' said the shepherd warmly.

'It is goodish mead,' assented Mrs Fennel, with an absence of enthusiasm which seemed to say that it was possible to buy praise for one's cellar at too heavy a price. 'It is trouble enough to make—and really I hardly think we shall make any more. For honey sells well, and we ourselves can make shift with a drop o' small mead and metheglin for common use from the comb-washings.'

'O, but you'll never have the heart!' reproachfully cried the stranger in cinder-grey, after taking up the mug a third time and setting it down empty. 'I love mead, when 'tis old like this, as I love to go to church o' Sundays, or to relieve the needy any day of the week.'

'Ha, ha, ha!' said the man in the chimney-corner, who, in spite of the taciturnity induced by the pipe of tobacco, could not or would not refrain from this slight testimony to his comrade's humour.

Now the old mead of those days, brewed of the purest first-year or maiden honey, four pounds to the gallon—with its due complement of white of eggs, cinnamon, ginger, cloves, mace, rosemary, yeast, and processes of working, bottling, and cellaring—tasted remarkably strong; but it did not taste so strong as it actually was. Hence, presently, the stranger in cinder-grey at the table, moved by its creeping influence, unbuttoned his waistcoat, threw himself back in his chair, spread his legs, and made his presence felt in various ways.

'Well, well, as I say,' he resumed, 'I am going to Casterbridge, and to Casterbridge I must go. I should have been almost there by this time; but the rain drove me into your dwelling, and I'm not sorry for it.'

'You don't live in Casterbridge?' said the shepherd.

'Not as yet; though I shortly mean to move there.'

'Going to set up in trade, perhaps?'

'No, no,' said the shepherd's wife. 'It is easy to see that the gentleman is rich, and don't want to work at anything.'

The cinder-grey stranger paused, as if to consider whether

he would accept that definition of himself. He presently rejected it by answering, 'Rich is not quite the word for me, dame. I do work, and I must work. And even if I only get to Casterbridge by midnight I must begin work there at eight tomorrow morning. Yes, het or wet, blow or snow, famine or sword, my day's work tomorrow must be done.'

'Poor man! Then, in spite o' seeming, you be worse off than we?' replied the shepherd's wife.

"Tis the nature of my trade, men and maidens. 'Tis the nature of my trade more than my poverty... But really and truly I must up and off, or I shan't get a lodging in the town.' However, the speaker did not move, and directly added, 'There's time for one more draught of friendship before I go; and I'd perform it at once if the mug were not dry.'

'Here's a mug o' small,' said Mrs Fennel. 'Small, we call it, though to be sure 'tis only the first wash o' the combs.'

'No,' said the stranger disdainfully. 'I won't spoil your first kindness by partaking o' your second.'

'Certainly not,' broke in Fennel. 'We don't increase and multiply every day, and I'll fill the mug again.' He went away to the dark place under the stairs where the barrel stood. The shepherdess followed him.

'Why should you do this?' she said reproachfully, as soon as they were alone. 'He's emptied it once, though it held enough for ten people; and now he's not contented wi' the small, but must needs call for more o' the strong! And a stranger unbeknown to any of us. For my part, I don't like the look o' the man at all.'

'But he's in the house, my honey; and 'tis a wet night, and a christening. Daze it, what's a cup of mead more or less? There'll be plenty more next bee-burning.'

'Very well—this time, then,' she answered, looking wistfully at the barrel. 'But what is the man's calling, and where is he one of; that he should come in and join us like this?'

'I don't know. I'll ask him again.'

The catastrophe of having the mug drained dry at one pull by the stranger in cinder-grey was effectually guarded against this time by Mrs Fennel. She poured out his allowance in a small cup, keeping the large one at a discreet distance from him. When he had tossed off his portion the shepherd renewed his inquiry about the stranger's occupation.

The latter did not immediately reply, and the man in the chimney-corner, with sudden demonstrativeness, said, 'Anybody may know my trade—I'm a wheelwright.'

'A very good trade for these parts,' said the shepherd.

'And anybody may know mine—if they've the sense to find it out,' said the stranger in cinder-grey.

'You may generally tell what a man is by his claws,' observed the hedge-carpenter, looking at his own hands. 'My fingers be as full of thorns as an old pin-cushion is of pins.'

The hands of the man in the chimney-corner instinctively sought the shade, and he gazed into the fire as he resumed his pipe. The man at the table took up the hedge-carpenter's remark, and added smartly, 'True; but the oddity of my trade is that, instead of setting a mark upon me, it sets a mark upon my customers.'

No observation being offered by anybody in elucidation of this enigma, the shepherd's wife once more called for a song. The same obstacles presented themselves as at the former time—one had no voice, another had forgotten the first verse. The stranger at the table, whose soul had now risen to a good working temperature, relieved the difficulty by exclaiming that, to start the company, he would sing himself. Thrusting one thumb into the armhole of his waistcoat, he waved the other hand in the air, and, with an extemporizing gaze at the shining sheep-crooks above the mantelpiece, began:

'O my trade it is the rarest one,
Simple shepherds all—
My trade is a sight to see;
For my customers I tie, and take them up on high,
And waft 'em to a far countree!'

The room was silent when he had finished the verse—with one exception, that of the man in the chimney-corner, who, at the singer's word, 'Chorus!' joined him in a deep bass voice of musical relish—

'And waft 'em to a far countree!'

Oliver Giles, John Pitcher the dairyman, the parish-clerk, the engaged man of fifty, the row of young women against the wall, seemed lost in thought not of the gayest kind. The shepherd looked meditatively on the ground, the shepherdess gazed keenly at the singer, and with some suspicion; she was doubting whether this stranger were merely singing an old song from recollection, or was composing one there and then for the occasion. All were as perplexed at the obscure revelation as the guests at Belshazzar's Feast, except the man in the chimney-corner, who quietly said, 'Second verse, stranger,' and smoked on.

The singer thoroughly moistened himself from his lips inwards, and went on with the next stanza as requested:

'My tools are but common ones,
Simple shepherds all—
My tools are no sight to see:
A little hempen string, and a post whereon to swing,
Are implements enough for me!'

Shepherd Fennel glanced round. There was no longer any doubt that the stranger was answering his question rhythmically. The guests one and all started back with suppressed exclamations. The young woman engaged to the man of fifty fainted halfway, and would have proceeded, but finding him wanting in alacrity for catching her she sat down trembling.

'O, he's the—!' whispered the people in the background, mentioning the name of an ominous public officer. 'He's come to do it! 'Tis to be at Casterbridge jail tomorrow—the man for sheep-stealing—the poor clockmaker we heard of; who used to live away at Shottsford and had no work to do—Timothy Summers, whose family were a-starving, and so he went out of Shottsford by the high-road, and took a sheep in open daylight, defying the farmer and the farmer's wife and the farmer's lad, and every man jack among 'em. He,' (and they nodded towards the stranger of the deadly trade) 'is come from up the country to do it because there's not enough to do in his own county-town, and he's got the place here now our own county man's dead; he's going to live in the same cottage under the prison wall.'

The stranger in cinder-grey took no notice of this whispered string of observations, but again wetted his lips. Seeing that his friend in the chimney-corner was the only one who reciprocated his joviality in any way, he held out his cup towards that appreciative comrade, who also held out his own. They clinked together, the eyes of the rest of the room hanging upon the singer's actions. He parted his lips for the third verse; but at that moment another knock was audible upon the door. This time the knock was faint and hesitating.

The company seemed scared; the shepherd looked with consternation towards the entrance, and it was with some effort that he resisted his alarmed wife's deprecatory glance, and uttered for the third time the welcoming words, 'Walk in!'

The door was gently opened, and another man stood upon the mat. He, like those who had preceded him, was a stranger. This time it was a short, small personage, of fair complexion, and dressed in a decent suit of dark clothes.

'Can you tell me the way to—?' he began: when, gazing

round the room to observe the nature of the company amongst whom he had fallen, his eyes lighted on the stranger in cinder-grey. It was just at the instant when the latter, who had thrown his mind into his song with such a will that he scarcely heeded the interruption, silenced all whispers and inquiries by bursting into his third verse:

'Tomorrow is my working day,
Simple shepherds all—
Tomorrow is a working day for me:
For the farmer's sheep is slain, and the lad who did it ta'en,
And on his soul may God ha' merc-y!'

The stranger in the chimney-corner, waving cups with the singer so heartily that his mead splashed over on the hearth, repeated in his bass voice as before:

'And on his soul may God ha' merc-y!'

All this time the third stranger had been standing in the doorway. Finding now that he did not come forward or go on speaking, the guests particularly regarded him. They noticed to their surprise that he stood before them the picture of abject terror—his knees trembling, his hand shaking so violently that the door-latch by which he supported himself rattled audibly: his white lips were parted, and his eyes fixed on the merry officer of justice in the middle of the room. A moment more and he had turned, closed the door, and fled.

'What a man can it be?' said the shepherd.

The rest, between the awfulness of their late discovery and the odd conduct of this third visitor, looked as if they knew not what to think, and said nothing. Instinctively they withdrew further and further from the grim gentleman in their midst, whom some of them seemed to take for the Prince of Darkness himself; till they formed a remote circle, an empty space of floor being left between them and him—

'...circulus, cujus centrum diabolus.'

The room was so silent—though there were more than twenty people in it—that nothing could be heard but the patter of the rain against the window-shutters, accompanied by the occasional hiss of a stray drop that fell down the chimney into the fire, and the steady puffing of the man in the corner, who had now resumed his pipe of long clay.

The stillness was unexpectedly broken. The distant sound of a gun reverberated through the air—apparently from the direction of the county-town.

'Be jiggered!' cried the stranger who had sung the song, jumping up.

'What does that mean?' asked several.

'A prisoner escaped from the jail—that's what it means.'

All listened. The sound was repeated, and none of them spoke but the man in the chimney-corner, who said quietly, 'I've often been told that in this county they fire a gun at such times; but I never heard it till now.'

'I wonder if it is *my* man?' murmured the personage in cinder-grey.

'Surely it is!' said the shepherd involuntarily. 'And surely we've zeed him! That little man who looked in at the door by now, and quivered like a leaf when he zeed ye and heard your song!'

'His teeth chattered, and the breath went out of his body,' said the dairyman.

'And his heart seemed to sink within him like a stone,' said Oliver Giles.

'And he bolted as if he'd been shot at,' said the hedge-carpenter.

'True—his teeth chattered, and his heart seemed to sink; and he bolted as if he'd been shot at,' slowly summed up the man in the chimney-corner.

'I didn't notice it,' remarked the hangman.

'We were all a-wondering what made him run off in such a fright,' faltered one of the women against the wall, 'and now 'tis explained!'

The firing of the alarm-gun went on at intervals, low and sullenly, and their suspicions became a certainty. The sinister gentleman in cinder-grey roused himself. 'Is there a constable here?' he asked, in thick tones. 'If so, let him step forward.'

The engaged man of fifty stepped quavering out from the wall, his betrothed beginning to sob on the back of the chair.

'You are a sworn constable?'

'I be, sir.'

'Then pursue the criminal at once, with assistance, and bring him back here. He can't have gone far.'

'I will, sir, I will—when I've got my staff. I'll go home and get it, and come sharp here, and start in a body.'

'Staff!—never mind your staff; the man'll be gone!'

'But I can't do nothing without my staff—can I, William, and John, and Charles Jake? No; for there's the king's royal crown a painted on en in yaller and gold, and the lion and the unicorn, so as when I raise en up and hit my prisoner, 'tis made a lawful blow thereby. I wouldn't 'tempt to take up a man without my staff—no, not I. If I hadn't the law to gie me courage, why, instead o' my taking up him he might take up me!'

'Now, I'm a king's man myself, and can give you authority enough for this,' said the formidable officer in grey. 'Now then, all of ye, be ready. Have ye any lanterns?'

'Yes—have ye any lanterns?—I demand it!' said the constable.

'And the rest of you able-bodied—'

'Able-bodied men—yes—the rest of ye!' said the constable.

'Have you some good stout staves and pitchforks—'

'Staves and pitchforks—in the name o' the law! And take 'em in yer hands and go in quest, and do as we in authority tell ye!'

Thus aroused, the men prepared to give chase. The evidence was, indeed, though circumstantial, so convincing, that but little argument was needed to show the shepherd's guests that after what they had seen it would look very much like connivance if they did not instantly pursue the unhappy third stranger, who could not as yet have gone more than a few hundred yards over such uneven country.

A shepherd is always well provided with lanterns; and, lighting these hastily, and with hurdle-staves in their hands, they poured out of the door, taking a direction along the crest of the hill, away from the town, the rain having fortunately a little abated.

Disturbed by the noise, or possibly by unpleasant dreams of her baptism, the child who had been christened began to cry heartbrokenly in the room overhead. These notes of grief came down through the chinks of the floor to the ears of the women below, who jumped up one by one, and seemed glad of the excuse to ascend and comfort the baby, for the incidents of the last half-hour greatly oppressed them. Thus in the space of two or three minutes the room on the ground floor was deserted quite.

But it was not for long. Hardly had the sound of footsteps died away when a man returned round the corner of the house from the direction the pursuers had taken. Peeping in at the door, and seeing nobody there, he entered leisurely. It was the stranger of the chimney-corner, who had gone out with the rest. The motive of his return was shown by his helping himself to a cut piece of skimmer-cake that lay on a ledge beside where he had sat, and which he had apparently forgotten to take with him. He also poured out half a cup more mead from the quantity that remained, ravenously eating and drinking these as he stood. He had not finished when another figure came in just as quietly—his friend in cinder-grey.

'O—you here?' said the latter, smiling. 'I thought you had gone to help in the capture.' And this speaker also revealed the object of his return by looking solicitously round for the fascinating mug of old mead.

'And I thought you had gone,' said the other, continuing his skimmer-cake with some effort.

'Well, on second thoughts, I felt there were enough without me,' said the first confidentially, 'and such a night as it is, too. Besides, 'tis the business o' the Government to take care of its criminals—not mine.'

'True; so it is. And I felt as you did, that there were enough without me.'

'I don't want to break my limbs running over the humps and hollows of this wild country.'

'Nor I neither, between you and me.'

'These shepherd-people are used to it—simple-minded souls, you know, stirred up to anything in a moment. They'll have him ready for me before the morning, and no trouble to me at all.'

'They'll have him, and we shall have saved ourselves all labour in the matter.'

'True, true. Well, my way is to Casterbridge; and 'tis as much as my legs will do to take me that far. Going the same way?'

'No, I am sorry to say! I have to get home over there,' (he nodded indefinitely to the right) 'and I feel as you do, that it is quite enough for my legs to do before bedtime.'

The other had by this time finished the mead in the mug, after which, shaking hands heartily at the door, and wishing each other well, they went their several ways.

In the meantime the company of pursuers had reached the end of the hog's-back elevation which dominated this part of the down. They had decided on no particular plan of action;

and, finding that the man of the baleful trade was no longer in their company, they seemed quite unable to form any such plan now. They descended in all directions down the hill, and straightway several of the party fell into the snare set by Nature for all misguided midnight ramblers over this part of the cretaceous formation. The 'lanchets', or flint slopes, which belted the escarpment at intervals of a dozen yards, took the less cautious ones unawares, and losing their footing on the rubbly steep they slid sharply downwards, the lanterns rolling from their hands to the bottom, and there lying on their sides till the horn was scorched through.

When they had again gathered themselves together, the shepherd, as the man who knew the country best, took the lead, and guided them round these treacherous inclines. The lanterns, which seemed rather to dazzle their eyes and warn the fugitive than to assist them in the exploration, were extinguished, due silence was observed; and in this more rational order they plunged into the vale. It was a grassy, briery, moist defile, affording some shelter to any person who had sought it; but the party perambulated it in vain, and ascended on the other side. Here they wandered apart, and after an interval closed together again to report progress.

At the second time of closing in they found themselves near a lonely ash, the single tree on this part of the coomb, probably sown there by a passing bird some fifty years before. And here, standing a little to one side of the trunk, as motionless as the trunk itself, appeared the man they were in quest of; his outline being well defined against the sky beyond. The band noiselessly drew up and faced him.

'Your money or your life!' said the constable sternly to the still figure.

'No, no,' whispered John Pitcher. "Tisn't our side ought to say that. That's the doctrine of vagabonds like him, and we be on the side of the law.'

'Well, well,' replied the constable impatiently; 'I must say something, mustn't I? and if you had all the weight o' this undertaking upon your mind, perhaps you'd say the wrong thing too!—Prisoner at the bar, surrender, in the name of the Father—the Crown, I mean!'

The man under the tree seemed now to notice them for the first time, and, giving them no opportunity whatever for exhibiting their courage, he strolled slowly towards them. He was, indeed, the little man, the third stranger; but his trepidation had in a great measure gone.

'Well, travellers,' he said, 'did I hear ye speak to me?'

'You did: you've got to come and be our prisoner at once!' said the constable. 'We arrest 'ee on the charge of not biding in Casterbridge jail in a decent proper manner to be hung tomorrow morning. Neighbours, do your duty, and seize the culpet!'

On hearing the charge, the man seemed enlightened, and, saying not another word, resigned himself with preternatural civility to the search-party, who, with their staves in their hands, surrounded him on all sides, and marched him back towards the shepherd's cottage.

It was eleven o'clock by the time they arrived. The light shining from the open door, a sound of men's voices within, proclaimed to them as they approached the house that some new events had arisen in their absence. On entering they discovered the shepherd's living-room to be invaded by two officers from Casterbridge jail, and a well-known magistrate who lived at the nearest country-seat, intelligence of the escape having become generally circulated.

'Gentlemen,' said the constable, 'I have brought back your man—not without risk and danger; but every one must do his duty! He is inside this circle of able-bodied persons, who have lent me useful aid, considering their ignorance of Crown work. Men, bring forward your prisoner!' And the third stranger was led to the light.

'Who is this?' said one of the officials.

'The man,' said the constable.

'Certainly not,' said the turnkey; and the first corroborated his statement.

'But how can it be otherwise?' asked the constable. 'Or why was he so terrified at sight o' the singing instrument of the law who sat there?' Here he related the strange behaviour of the third stranger on entering the house during the hangman's song.

'Can't understand it,' said the officer coolly. 'All I know is that it is not the condemned man. He's quite a different character from this one; a gauntish fellow, with dark hair and eyes, rather good-looking, and with a musical bass voice that if you heard it once you'd never mistake as long as you lived.'

'Why, souls—'twas the man in the chimney-corner!'

'Hey—what?' said the magistrate, coming forward after inquiring particulars from the shepherd in the background. 'Haven't you got the man after all?'

'Well, sir,' said the constable, 'he's the man we were in search of, that's true; and yet he's not the man we were in search of. For the man we were in search of was not the man we wanted, sir, if you understand my everyday way; for 'twas the man in the chimney-corner!'

'A pretty kettle of fish altogether!' said the magistrate. 'You had better start for the other man at once.'

The prisoner now spoke for the first time. The mention of the man in the chimney-corner seemed to have moved him as nothing else could do. 'Sir,' he said, stepping forward to the magistrate, 'take no more trouble about me. The time is come when I may as well speak. I have done nothing; my crime is that the condemned man is my brother. Early this afternoon I left home at Shottsford to tramp it all the way to Casterbridge jail to bid him farewell. I was benighted, and called here to rest and ask the way. When I opened the door I saw before me the very man, my brother, that I thought to see in the condemned cell at Casterbridge. He was in this chimney-corner; and jammed close to him, so that he could not have got out if he had tried, was the executioner who'd come to take his life, singing a song about it and not knowing that it was his victim who was close by, joining in to save appearances. My brother looked a glance of agony at me, and I knew he meant, "Don't reveal what you see; my life depends on it." I was so terror-struck that I could hardly stand, and, not knowing what I did, I turned and hurried away.'

The narrator's manner and tone had the stamp of truth, and his story made a great impression on all around. 'And do you know where your brother is at the present time?' asked the magistrate.

'I do not. I have never seen him since I closed this door.'

'I can testify to that, for we've been between ye ever since,' said the constable.

'Where does he think to fly to?—what is his occupation?'

'He's a watch-and-clock-maker, sir.'

''A said 'a was a wheelwright—a wicked rogue,' said the constable.

'The wheels of clocks and watches he meant, no doubt,' said Shepherd Fennel. 'I thought his hands were palish for's trade.'

'Well, it appears to me that nothing can be gained by retaining this poor man in custody,' said the magistrate; 'your business lies with the other, unquestionably.'

And so the little man was released offhand; but he looked nothing the less sad on that account, it being beyond the power of magistrate or constable to raze out the written troubles in his brain, for they concerned another whom he regarded with more solicitude than himself. When this was done, and the man had gone his way, the night was found to be so far advanced that it was deemed useless to renew the search before the next morning.

Next day, accordingly, the quest for the clever sheep-stealer became general and keen, to all appearance at least. But the intended punishment was cruelly disproportioned to the transgression, and the sympathy of a great many country-folk in that district was strongly on the side of the fugitive. Moreover, his marvellous coolness and daring in hob-and-nobbing with the hangman, under the unprecedented circumstances of the shepherd's party, won their admiration. So that it may be questioned if all those who ostensibly made themselves so busy in exploring woods and fields and lanes were quite so thorough when it came to the private examination of their own lofts and outhouses. Stories were afloat of a mysterious figure being occasionally seen in some old overgrown trackway or other, remote from turnpike roads; but when a search was instituted in any of these suspected quarters nobody was found. Thus the days and weeks passed without tidings.

In brief, the bass-voiced man of the chimney-corner was never recaptured. Some said that he went across the sea, others that he did not, but buried himself in the depths of a populous city. At any rate, the gentleman in cinder-grey never did his morning's work at Casterbridge, nor met anywhere at all, for business purposes, the genial comrade with whom he had passed an hour of relaxation in the lonely house on the coomb.

The grass has long been green on the graves of Shepherd Fennel and his frugal wife; the guests who made up the christening party have mainly followed their entertainers to the tomb; the baby in whose honour they all had met is a matron in the sere and yellow leaf. But the arrival of the three strangers at the shepherd's that night, and the details connected therewith, is a story as well known as ever in the country about Higher Crowstairs.

4

TO PLEASE HIS WIFE

I

The interior of St. James's Church, in Havenpool Town, was slowly darkening under the close clouds of a winter afternoon. It was Sunday: service had just ended, the face of the parson in the pulpit was buried in his hands, and the congregation, with a cheerful sigh of release, were rising from their knees to depart.

For the moment the stillness was so complete that the surging of the sea could be heard outside the harbour-bar. Then it was broken by the footsteps of the clerk going towards the west door to open it in the usual manner for the exit of the assembly. Before, however, he had reached the doorway, the latch was lifted from without, and the dark figure of a man in a sailor's garb appeared against the light.

The clerk stepped aside, the sailor closed the door gently behind him, and advanced up the nave till he stood at the chancel-step. The parson looked up from the private little prayer which, after so many for the parish, he quite fairly took for himself; rose to his feet, and stared at the intruder.

'I beg your pardon, sir,' said the sailor, addressing the minister in a voice distinctly audible to all the congregation.

'I have come here to offer thanks for my narrow escape from shipwreck. I am given to understand that it is a proper thing to do, if you have no objection?'

The parson, after a moment's pause, said hesitatingly, 'I have no objection; certainly. It is usual to mention any such wish before service, so that the proper words may be used in the General Thanksgiving. But, if you wish, we can read from the form for use after a storm at sea.'

'Ay, sure; I ain't particular,' said the sailor.

The clerk thereupon directed the sailor to the page in the prayer-book where the collect of thanksgiving would be found, and the rector began reading it, the sailor kneeling where he stood, and repeating it after him word by word in a distinct voice. The people, who had remained agape and motionless at the proceeding, mechanically knelt down likewise; but they continued to regard the isolated form of the sailor who, in the precise middle of the chancel-step, remained fixed on his knees, facing the east, his hat beside him, his hands joined, and he quite unconscious of his appearance in their regard.

When his thanksgiving had come to an end he rose; the people rose also, and all went out of church together. As soon as the sailor emerged, so that the remaining daylight fell upon his face, old inhabitants began to recognize him as no other than Shadrach Jolliffe, a young man who had not been seen at Havenpool for several years. A son of the town, his parents had died when he was quite young, on which account he had early gone to sea, in the Newfoundland trade.

He talked with this and that townsman as he walked, informing them that, since leaving his native place years before, he had become captain and owner of a small coasting-ketch, which had providentially been saved from the gale as well as himself. Presently he drew near to two girls who were going out of the churchyard in front of him; they had been sitting in the nave at his entry, and had watched his doings with deep interest, afterwards discussing him as they moved out of church together. One was a slight and gentle creature, the other a tall, large-framed, deliberative girl. Captain Jolliffe regarded the loose curls of their hair, their backs and shoulders, down to their heels, for some time.

'Who may them two maids be?' he whispered to his neighbour.

'The little one is Emily Hanning; the tall one Joanna Phippard.'

'Ah! I recollect 'em now, to be sure.'

He advanced to their elbow, and genially stole a gaze at them.

'Emily, you don't know me?' said the sailor, turning his beaming brown eyes on her.

'I think I do, Mr Jolliffe,' said Emily shyly.

The other girl looked straight at him with her dark eyes.

'The face of Miss Joanna I don't call to mind so well,' he continued. 'But I know her beginnings and kindred.'

They walked and talked together, Jolliffe narrating particulars of his late narrow escape, till they reached the corner of Sloop Lane, in which Emily Hanning dwelt, when, with a nod and smile, she left them. Soon the sailor parted also from Joanna, and, having no especial errand or appointment, turned back towards Emily's house. She lived with her father, who called himself an accountant, the daughter, however, keeping a little stationery shop as a supplemental provision for the gaps of his somewhat uncertain business. On entering Jolliffe found father and daughter about to begin tea.

'O, I didn't know it was teatime,' he said. 'Ay, I'll have a cup with much pleasure.'

He remained to tea and long afterwards, telling more tales of his seafaring life. Several neighbours called to listen, and were asked to come in. Somehow Emily Hanning lost her heart to the sailor that Sunday night, and in the course of a week or two there was a tender understanding between them.

One moonlight evening in the next month Shadrach was ascending out of the town by the long straight road eastward, to an elevated suburb where the more fashionable houses stood—if anything near this ancient port could be called fashionable—when he saw a figure before him whom, from her manner of glancing back, he took to be Emily. But, on coming up, he found she was Joanna Phippard. He gave a gallant greeting, and walked beside her.

'Go along,' she said, 'or Emily will be jealous!'

He seemed not to like the suggestion, and remained. What was said and what was done on that walk never could be clearly recollected by Shadrach; but in some way or other Joanna contrived to wean him away from her gentler and younger rival. From that week onwards, Jolliffe was seen more and more in the wake of Joanna Phippard and less in the company of Emily; and it was soon rumoured about the quay that old Jolliffe's son, who had come home from sea, was going to be married to the former young woman, to the great disappointment of the latter.

Just after this report had gone about, Joanna dressed herself for a walk one morning, and started for Emily's house in the little cross-street. Intelligence of the deep sorrow of her friend on account of the loss of Shadrach had reached her ears also, and her conscience reproached her for winning him away.

Joanna was not altogether satisfied with the sailor. She liked his attentions, and she coveted the dignity of matrimony; but she had never been deeply in love with Jolliffe. For one thing, she was ambitious, and socially his position was hardly so good as her own, and there was always the chance of an attractive woman mating considerably above her. It had long been in her mind that she would not strongly object to give him back again to Emily if her friend felt so very badly about him. To this end she had written a letter of renunciation to Shadrach, which letter she carried in her hand, intending to send it if personal observation of Emily convinced her that her friend was suffering.

Joanna entered Sloop Lane and stepped down into the stationery shop, which was below the pavement level. Emily's father was never at home at this hour of the day, and it seemed as though Emily were not at home either, for the visitor could make nobody hear. Customers came so seldom hither that a five minutes' absence of the proprietor counted for little. Joanna waited in the little shop, where Emily had tastefully set out—as women can—articles in themselves of slight value, so as to obscure the meagreness of the stock-in-trade; till she saw a figure pausing without the window apparently absorbed in the contemplation of the sixpenny books, packets of paper, and prints hung on a string. It was Captain Shadrach Jolliffe, peering in to ascertain if Emily were there alone. Moved by an impulse of reluctance to meet him in a spot which breathed of Emily, Joanna slipped through the door that communicated with the parlour at the back. She had frequently done so before, for in her friendship with Emily she had the freedom of the house without ceremony.

Jolliffe entered the shop. Through the thin blind which screened the glass partition she could see that he was disappointed at not finding Emily there. He was about to go out again, when Emily's form darkened the doorway, hastening home from some errand. At sight of Jolliffe she started back as if she would have gone out again.

'Don't run away, Emily; don't!' said he. 'What can make ye afraid?'

'I'm not afraid, Captain Jolliffe. Only—only I saw you all of a sudden, and—it made me jump!' Her voice showed that her heart had jumped even more than the rest of her.

'I just called as I was passing,' he said.

'For some paper?' She hastened behind the counter.

'No, no, Emily; why do ye get behind there? Why not stay by me? You seem to hate me.'

'I don't hate you. How can I?'

'Then come out, so that we can talk like Christians.'

Emily obeyed with a fitful laugh, till she stood again beside him in the open part of the shop.

'There's a dear,' he said.

'You mustn't say that, Captain Jolliffe; because the words belong to somebody else.'

'Ah! I know what you mean. But, Emily, upon my life I didn't know till this morning that you cared one bit about me, or I should not have done as I have done. I have the best of feelings for Joanna, but I know that from the beginning she hasn't cared for me more than in a friendly way; and I see now the one I ought to have asked to be my wife. You know, Emily, when a man comes home from sea after a long voyage he's as blind as a bat—he can't see who's who in women. They are all alike to him, beautiful creatures, and he takes the first that comes easy, without thinking if she loves him, or if he might not soon love another better than her. From the first I inclined to you most, but you were so backward and shy that I thought you didn't want me to bother 'ee, and so I went to Joanna.'

'Don't say any more, Mr Jolliffe, don't!' said she, choking. 'You are going to marry Joanna next month, and it is wrong to—to—'

'O, Emily, my darling!' he cried, and clasped her little figure in his arms before she was aware.

Joanna, behind the curtain, turned pale, tried to withdraw her eyes, but could not.

'It is only you I love as a man ought to love the woman he is going to marry; and I know this from what Joanna has said, that she will willingly let me off! She wants to marry higher I know, and only said "Yes" to me out of kindness. A fine, tall girl like her isn't the sort for a plain sailor's wife: you be the best suited for that.'

He kissed her and kissed her again, her flexible form quivering in the agitation of his embrace.

'I wonder—are you sure—Joanna is going to break off with you? O, are you sure? Because—'

'I know she would not wish to make us miserable. She will release me.'

'O, I hope—I hope she will! Don't stay any longer, Captain Jolliffe!'

He lingered, however, till a customer came for a penny stick of sealing-wax, and then he withdrew.

Green envy had overspread Joanna at the scene. She looked about for a way of escape. To get out without Emily's knowledge of her visit was indispensable. She crept from the parlour into the passage, and thence to the front door of the house, where she let herself noiselessly into the street.

The sight of that caress had reversed all her resolutions. She could not let Shadrach go. Reaching home she burnt the letter, and told her mother that if Captain Jolliffe called she was too unwell to see him.

Shadrach, however, did not call. He sent her a note expressing in simple language the state of his feelings; and asked to be allowed to take advantage of the hints she had given him that her affection, too, was little more than friendly, by cancelling the engagement.

Looking out upon the harbour and the island beyond he waited and waited in his lodgings for an answer that did not come. The suspense grew to be so intolerable that after dark he went up the High Street. He could not resist calling at Joanna's to learn his fate.

Her mother said her daughter was too unwell to see him, and to his questioning admitted that it was in consequence of a letter received from himself; which had distressed her deeply.

'You know what it was about, perhaps, Mrs Phippard?' he said.

Mrs Phippard owned that she did, adding that it put them in a very painful position. Thereupon Shadrach, fearing that he had been guilty of an enormity, explained that if his letter had pained Joanna it must be owing to a misunderstanding, since he had thought it would be a relief to her. If otherwise, he would hold himself bound by his word, and she was to think of the letter as never having been written.

Next morning he received an oral message from the young woman, asking him to fetch her home from a meeting that evening. This he did, and while walking from the Town Hall to her door, with her hand in his arm, she said:

'It is all the same as before between us, isn't it, Shadrach? Your letter was sent in mistake?'

'It is all the same as before,' he answered, 'if you say it must be.'

'I wish it to be,' she murmured, with hard lineaments, as she thought of Emily.

Shadrach was a religious and scrupulous man, who respected his word as his life. Shortly afterwards the wedding took place, Jolliffe having conveyed to Emily as gently as possible the error he had fallen into when estimating Joanna's mood as one of indifference.

II

A month after the marriage Joanna's mother died, and the couple were obliged to turn their attention to very practical matters. Now that she was left without a parent, Joanna could not bear the notion of her husband going to sea again, but the question was, What could he do at home? They finally decided to take on a grocer's shop in High Street, the goodwill and stock of which were waiting to be disposed of at that time. Shadrach knew nothing of shopkeeping, and Joanna very little, but they hoped to learn.

To the management of this grocery business they now devoted all their energies, and continued to conduct it for many succeeding years, without great success. Two sons were born to them, whom their mother loved to idolatry, although she had never passionately loved her husband; and she lavished upon them all her forethought and care. But the shop did not thrive, and the large dreams she had entertained of her sons' education and career became attenuated in the face of realities. Their schooling was of the plainest, but, being by the sea, they grew alert in all such nautical arts and enterprises as were attractive to their age.

The great interest of the Jolliffes' married life, outside their own immediate household, had lain in the marriage of Emily. By one of those odd chances which lead those that lurk in unexpected corners to be discovered, while the obvious are passed by, the gentle girl had been seen and loved by a thriving merchant of the town, a widower, some years older than herself, though still in the prime of life. At first Emily had declared that she never, never could marry anyone; but Mr Lester had quietly persevered, and had at last won her reluctant assent. Two children also were the fruits of this union, and, as they grew and prospered, Emily declared that she had never supposed that she could live to be so happy.

The worthy merchant's home, one of those large, substantial brick mansions frequently jammed up in old-fashioned towns, faced directly on the High Street, nearly opposite to the grocery shop of the Jolliffes, and it now became the pain of Joanna to behold the woman whose place she had usurped out of pure covetousness, looking down from her position of comparative wealth upon the humble shop-window with its dusty sugar-loaves, heaps of raisins, and canisters of tea, over which it was her own lot to preside. The business having so dwindled, Joanna was obliged to serve in the shop herself; and it galled and mortified her that Emily Lester, sitting in her large drawing-room over the way, could witness her own dancings up and down behind the counter at the beck and call of wretched twopenny customers, whose patronage she was driven to welcome gladly: persons to whom she was compelled to be civil in the street, while Emily was bounding along with her children and her governess, and conversing with the genteelest people of the town and neighbourhood. This was what she had gained by not letting Shadrach Jolliffe, whom she had so faintly loved, carry his affection elsewhere.

Shadrach was a good and honest man, and he had been faithful to her in heart and in deed. Time had clipped the wings of his love for Emily in his devotion to the mother of his boys: he had quite lived down that impulsive earlier fancy, and Emily had become in his regard nothing more than a friend. It was the same with Emily's feelings for him. Possibly, had she found the least cause for jealousy, Joanna would almost have been better satisfied. It was in the absolute acquiescence of Emily and Shadrach in the results she herself had contrived that her discontent found nourishment.

Shadrach was not endowed with the narrow shrewdness necessary for developing a retail business in the face of many competitors. Did a customer inquire if the grocer could really recommend the wondrous substitute for eggs which a persevering bagman had forced into his stock, he would answer that 'when you did not put eggs into a pudding it was difficult to taste them there'; and when he was asked if his 'real Mocha coffee' was real Mocha, he would say grimly, 'as understood in small shops'.

One summer day, when the big brick house opposite was reflecting the oppressive sun's heat into the shop, and nobody was present but husband and wife, Joanna looked across at Emily's door, where a wealthy visitor's carriage had drawn up. Traces of patronage had been visible in Emily's manner of late.

'Shadrach, the truth is, you are not a businessman,' his wife sadly murmured. 'You were not brought up to shopkeeping, and it is impossible for a man to make a fortune at an occupation he has jumped into, as you did into this.'

Jolliffe agreed with her, in this as in everything else.

'Not that I care a rope's end about making a fortune,' he said cheerfully. 'I am happy enough, and we can rub on somehow.'

She looked again at the great house through the screen of bottled pickles.

'Rub on—yes,' she said bitterly. 'But see how well off Emmy Lester is, who used to be so poor! Her boys will go to College, no doubt; and think of yours—obliged to go to the Parish School!'

Shadrach's thoughts had flown to Emily.

'Nobody,' he said good-humouredly, 'ever did Emily a better turn than you did, Joanna, when you warned her off me and put an end to that little simpering nonsense between us, so as to leave it in her power to say "Aye" to Lester when he came along.' This almost maddened her.

'Don't speak of bygones!' she implored, in stern sadness. 'But think, for the boys' and my sake, if not for your own, what are we to do to get richer?'

'Well,' he said, becoming serious, 'to tell the truth, I have always felt myself unfit for this business, though I've never liked to say so. I seem to want more room for sprawling; a more open space to strike out in than here among friends and neighbours. I could get rich as well as any man, if I tried my own way.'

'I wish you would! What is your way?'

'To go to sea again.'

She had been the very one to keep him at home, hating the semi-widowed existence of sailors' wives. But her ambition checked her instincts now, and she said: 'Do you think success really lies that way?'

'I am sure it lies in no other.'

'Do you want to go, Shadrach?'

'Not for the pleasure of it, I can tell 'ee. There's no such pleasure at sea, Joanna, as I can find in my back parlour here. To speak honest, I have no love for the brine. I never had much. But if it comes to a question of a fortune for you and the lads, it is another thing. That's the only way to it for one born and bred a seafarer as I.'

'Would it take long to earn?'

'Well, that depends; perhaps not.'

The next morning Shadrach pulled from a chest of drawers the nautical jacket he had worn during the first months of his return, brushed out the moths, donned it, and walked down to the quay. The port still did a fair business in the Newfoundland trade, though not so much as formerly.

It was not long after this that he invested all he possessed in purchasing a part-ownership in a brig, of which he was appointed captain. A few months were passed in coast-trading, during which interval Shadrach wore off the land-rust that had accumulated upon him in his grocery phase; and in the spring the brig sailed for Newfoundland.

Joanna lived on at home with her sons, who were now growing up into strong lads, and occupying themselves in various ways about the harbour and quay.

'Never mind, let them work a little,' their fond mother said to herself. 'Our necessities compel it now, but when Shadrach comes home they will be only seventeen and eighteen, and they shall be removed from the port, and their education thoroughly taken in hand by a tutor; and with the money they'll have they will perhaps be as near to gentlemen as Emmy Lester's precious two, with their algebra and their Latin!'

The date for Shadrach's return drew near and arrived, and he did not appear. Joanna was assured that there was no cause for anxiety, sailing-ships being so uncertain in their coming; which assurance proved to be well grounded, for late one wet evening, about a month after the calculated time, the ship was announced as at hand, and presently the slip-slop step of Shadrach the sailor sounded in the passage, and he entered. The boys had gone out and had missed him, and Joanna was sitting alone.

As soon as the first emotion of reunion between the couple had passed, Jolliffe explained the delay as owing to a small speculative contract, which had produced good results.

'I was determined not to disappoint 'ee,' he said; 'and I think you'll own that I haven't!'

With this he pulled out an enormous canvas bag, full and rotund as the money-bag of the giant whom Jack slew, untied it, and shook the contents out into her lap as she sat in her low chair by the fire. A mass of sovereigns and guineas (there were guineas on the earth in those days) fell into her lap with a sudden thud, weighing down her gown to the floor.

'There!' said Shadrach complacently. 'I told 'ee, dear, I'd do it; and have I done it or no?'

Somehow her face, after the first excitement of possession, did not retain its glory.

'It is a lot of gold, indeed,' she said. 'And—is this *all*?'

'All? Why, dear Joanna, do you know you can count to three

hundred in that heap? It is a fortune!'

'Yes—yes. A fortune—judged by sea; but judged by land—'

However, she banished considerations of the money for the nonce. Soon the boys came in, and next Sunday Shadrach returned thanks to God—this time by the more ordinary channel of the italics in the General Thanksgiving. But a few days after, when the question of investing the money arose, he remarked that she did not seem so satisfied as he had hoped.

'Well you see, Shadrach,' she answered, 'we count by hundreds; *they* count by thousands,' (nodding towards the other side of the street). 'They have set up a carriage and pair since you left.'

'O, have they?'

'My dear Shadrach, you don't know how the world moves. However, we'll do the best we can with it. But they are rich, and we are poor still!'

The greater part of a year was desultorily spent. She moved sadly about the house and shop, and the boys were still occupying themselves in and around the harbour.

'Joanna,' he said, one day, 'I see by your movements that it is not enough.'

'It is not enough,' said she. 'My boys will have to live by steering the ships that the Lesters own; and I was once above her!'

Jolliffe was not an argumentative man, and he only murmured that he thought he would make another voyage.

He meditated for several days, and coming home from the quay one afternoon said suddenly:

'I could do it for 'ee, dear, in one more trip, for certain, if—if—'

'Do what, Shadrach?'

'Enable 'ee to count by thousands instead of hundreds.'

'If what?'

'If I might take the boys.'

She turned pale.

'Don't say that, Shadrach,' she answered hastily.

'Why?'

'I don't like to hear it! There's danger at sea. I want them to be something genteel, and no danger to them. I couldn't let them risk their lives at sea. O, I couldn't ever, ever!'

'Very well, dear, it shan't be done.'

Next day, after a silence, she asked a question:

'If they were to go with you it would make a great deal of difference, I suppose, to the profit?'

'"Twould treble what I should get from the venture single-handed. Under my eye they would be as good as two more of myself.'

Later on she said: 'Tell me more about this.'

'Well, the boys are almost as clever as master-mariners in handling a craft, upon my life! There isn't a more cranky place in the Northern Seas than about the sandbanks of this harbour, and they've practised here from their infancy. And they are so steady. I couldn't get their steadiness and their trustworthiness in half a dozen men twice their age.'

'And is it *very* dangerous at sea; now, too, there are rumours of war?' she asked uneasily.

'O, well, there be risks. Still...'

The idea grew and magnified, and the mother's heart was crushed and stifled by it. Emily was growing *too* patronizing; it could not be borne. Shadrach's wife could not help nagging him about their comparative poverty. The young men, amiable as their father, when spoken to on the subject of a voyage of enterprise, were quite willing to embark; and though they, like their father, had no great love for the sea, they became quite enthusiastic when the proposal was detailed.

Everything now hung upon their mother's assent. She

withheld it long, but at last gave the word: the young men might accompany their father. Shadrach was unusually cheerful about it: Heaven had preserved him hitherto, and he had uttered his thanks. God would not forsake those who were faithful to him.

All that the Jolliffes possessed in the world was put into the enterprise. The grocery stock was pared down to the least that possibly could afford a bare sustenance to Joanna during the absence, which was to last through the usual 'Newf'nland spell'. How she would endure the weary time she hardly knew, for the boys had been with her formerly; but she nerved herself for the trial.

The ship was laden with boots and shoes, ready-made clothing, fishing-tackle, butter, cheese, cordage, sailcloth, and many other commodities; and was to bring back oil, furs, skins, fish, cranberries, and what else came to hand. But much trading to other ports was to be undertaken between the voyages out and homeward, and thereby much money made.

III

The brig sailed on a Monday morning in spring; but Joanna did not witness its departure. She could not bear the sight that she had been the means of bringing about. Knowing this, her husband told her overnight that they were to sail some time before noon next day, hence when, awakening at five the next morning, she heard them bustling about downstairs, she did not hasten to descend, but lay trying to nerve herself for the parting, imagining they would leave about nine, as her husband had done on his previous voyage. When she did descend she beheld words chalked upon the sloping face of the bureau; but no husband or sons. In the hastily-scrawled lines Shadrach said they had gone off thus not to pain her by a leave-taking; and the sons had chalked under his words: 'Good-bye, mother!'

She rushed to the quay, and looked down the harbour towards the blue rim of the sea, but she could only see the masts and bulging sails of the *Joanna*; no human figures. "'Tis I have sent them!' she said wildly, and burst into tears. In the house the chalked 'Good-bye' nearly broke her heart. But when she had re-entered the front room, and looked across at Emily's, a gleam of triumph lit her thin face at her anticipated release from the thraldom of subservience.

To do Emily Lester justice, her assumption of superiority was mainly a figment of Joanna's brain. That the circumstances of the merchant's wife were more luxurious than Joanna's, the former could not conceal; though whenever the two met, which was not very often now, Emily endeavoured to subdue the difference by every means in her power.

The first summer lapsed away; and Joanna meagrely maintained herself by the shop, which now consisted of little more than a window and a counter. Emily was, in truth, her only large customer; and Mrs Lester's kindly readiness to buy anything and everything without questioning the quality had a sting of bitterness in it, for it was the uncritical attitude of a patron, and almost of a donor. The long dreary winter moved on; the face of the bureau had been turned to the wall to protect the chalked words of farewell, for Joanna could never bring herself to rub them out; and she often glanced at them with wet eyes. Emily's handsome boys came home for the Christmas holidays; the University was talked of for them; and still Joanna subsisted as it were with held breath, like a person submerged. Only one summer more, and the 'spell' would end. Towards the close of the time Emily called on her quondam friend. She had heard that Joanna began to feel anxious; she had received no letter from husband or sons for some months. Emily's silks rustled arrogantly when, in response to Joanna's almost dumb invitation, she squeezed through the opening of the counter and into the parlour behind the shop.

'*You* are all success, and *I* am all the other way!' said Joanna.

'But why do you think so?' said Emily. 'They are to bring back a fortune, I hear.'

'Ah! Will they come? The doubt is more than a woman can bear. All three in one ship—think of that! And I have not heard of them for months!'

'But the time is not up. You should not meet misfortune halfway.'

'Nothing will repay me for the grief of their absence!'

'Then why did you let them go? You were doing fairly well.'

'I made them go!' she said, turning vehemently upon Emily. 'And I'll tell you why! I could not bear that we should be only muddling on, and you so rich and thriving! Now I have told you, and you may hate me if you will!'

'I shall never hate you, Joanna.'

And she proved the truth of her words afterwards. The end of autumn came, and the brig should have been in port; but nothing like the *Joanna* appeared in the channel between the sands. It was now really time to be uneasy. Joanna Jolliffe sat by the fire, and every gust of wind caused her a cold thrill. She had always feared and detested the sea; to her it was a treacherous, restless, slimy creature, glorying in the griefs of women. 'Still,' she said, 'they *must* come!'

She recalled to her mind that Shadrach had said before starting that if they returned safe and sound, with success crowning their enterprise, he would go as he had gone after his shipwreck, and kneel with his sons in the church, and offer sincere thanks for their deliverance. She went to church regularly morning and afternoon, and sat in the most forward pew, nearest the chancel-step. Her eyes were mostly fixed on that step, where Shadrach had knelt in the bloom of his young manhood: she knew to an inch the spot which his knees had pressed twenty winters before; his outline as he had knelt, his hat on the step beside him. God was good. Surely her husband must kneel there again: a son on each side as he had said; George just here, Jim just there. By long watching the spot as she worshipped it became as if she saw the three returned ones there kneeling; the two slim outlines of her boys, the more bulky form between them; their hands clasped, their heads shaped against the eastern wall. The fancy grew almost to an hallucination: she could never turn her worn eyes to the step without seeing them there.

Nevertheless they did not come. Heaven was merciful, but it was not yet pleased to relieve her soul. This was her purgation for the sin of making them the slaves of her ambition. But it became more than purgation soon, and her mood approached despair. Months had passed since the brig had been due, but it had not returned.

Joanna was always hearing or seeing evidences of their arrival. When on the hill behind the port, whence a view of the open Channel could be obtained, she felt sure that a little speck on the horizon, breaking the eternally level waste of waters southward, was the truck of the *Joanna's* mainmast. Or when indoors, a shout or excitement of any kind at the corner of the Town Cellar, where the High Street joined the Quay, caused her to spring to her feet and cry: "'Tis they!'

But it was not. The visionary forms knelt every Sunday afternoon on the chancel-step, but not the real. Her shop had, as it were, eaten itself hollow. In the apathy which had resulted from her loneliness and grief she had ceased to take in the smallest supplies, and thus had sent away her last customer.

In this strait Emily Lester tried by every means in her power to aid the afflicted woman; but she met with constant repulses.

'I don't like you! I can't bear to see you!' Joanna would whisper hoarsely when Emily came to her and made advances.

'But I want to help and soothe you, Joanna,' Emily would say.

'You are a lady, with a rich husband and fine sons! What can you want with a bereaved crone like me!'

'Joanna, I want this: I want you to come and live in my house, and not stay alone in this dismal place any longer.'

'And suppose they come and don't find me at home? You wish to separate me and mine! No, I'll stay here. I don't like you, and I can't thank you, whatever kindness you do me!'

However, as time went on Joanna could not afford to pay the rent of the shop and house without an income. She was assured that all hope of the return of Shadrach and his sons was vain, and she reluctantly consented to accept the asylum of the Lesters' house. Here she was allotted a room of her own on the second floor, and went and came as she chose, without contact with the family. Her hair greyed and whitened, deep lines channelled her forehead, and her form grew gaunt and stooping. But she still expected the lost ones, and when she met Emily on the staircase she would say morosely: 'I know why you've got me here! They'll come, and be disappointed at not finding me at home, and perhaps go away again; and then you'll be revenged for my taking Shadrach away from 'ee!'

Emily Lester bore these reproaches from the grief-stricken soul. She was sure—all the people of Havenpool were sure—that Shadrach and his sons could not return. For years the vessel had been given up as lost.

Nevertheless, when awakened at night by any noise, Joanna would rise from bed and glance at the shop opposite by the light from the flickering lamp, to make sure it was not they.

It was a damp and dark December night, six years after the departure of the brig *Joanna*. The wind was from the sea, and brought up a fishy mist which mopped the face like moist flannel. Joanna had prayed her usual prayer for the absent ones with more fervour and confidence than she had felt for months, and had fallen asleep about eleven. It must have been between one and two when she suddenly started up. She had certainly heard steps in the street, and the voices of Shadrach and her sons calling at the door of the grocery shop. She sprang out of bed, and, hardly knowing what clothing she dragged on herself, hastened down Emily's large and carpeted staircase, put the candle on the hall-table, unfastened the bolts and chain, and stepped into the street. The mist, blowing up the street from the Quay, hindered her seeing the shop, although it was so near; but she had crossed to it in a moment. How was it? Nobody stood there. The wretched woman walked wildly up and down with her bare feet—there was not a soul. She returned and knocked with all her might at the door which had once been her own—they might have been admitted for the night, unwilling to disturb her till the morning.

It was not till several minutes had elapsed that the young man who now kept the shop looked out of an upper window, and saw the skeleton of something human standing below half-dressed.

'Has anybody come?' asked the form.

'O, Mrs Jolliffe, I didn't know it was you,' said the young man kindly, for he was aware how her baseless expectations moved her. 'No; nobody has come.'

5

THE FIDDLER OF THE REELS

'Talking of Exhibitions, World's Fairs, and what not,' said the old gentleman, 'I would not go round the corner to see a dozen of them nowadays. The only exhibition that ever made, or ever will make, any impression upon my imagination was the first of the series, the parent of them all, and now a thing of old times—the Great Exhibition of 1851, in Hyde Park, London. None of the younger generation can realize the sense of novelty it produced in us who were then in our prime. A noun substantive went so far as to become an adjective in honour of the occasion. It was 'exhibition' hat, 'exhibition' razor-strop, 'exhibition' watch; nay, even 'exhibition' weather, 'exhibition' spirits, sweethearts, babies, wives—for the time.

'For South Wessex, the year formed in many ways an extraordinary chronological frontier or transit-line, at which there occurred what one might call a precipice in Time. As in a geological 'fault' we had presented to us a sudden bringing of ancient and modern into absolute contact, such as probably in no other single year since the Conquest was ever witnessed in this part of the country.'

These observations led us onward to talk of the different personages, gentle and simple, who lived and moved within our narrow and peaceful horizon at that time; and of three people in particular, whose queer little history was oddly touched at points by the Exhibition, more concerned with it than that of anybody else who dwelt in those outlying shades of the world, Stickleford, Mellstock, and Egdon. First prominence among these three came Wat Ollamoor—if that were his real name—whom the seniors in our party had known well.

He was a woman's man, they said,—supremely so—externally little else. To men he was not attractive; perhaps a little repulsive at times. Musician, dandy, and company-man in practice; veterinary surgeon in theory, he lodged awhile in Mellstock village, coming from nobody knew where; though some said his first appearance in this neighbourhood had been as fiddle-player in a show at Greenhill Fair.

Many a worthy villager envied him his power over unsophisticated maidenhood—power which seemed sometimes to have a touch of the weird and wizardly in it. Personally he was not ill-favoured, though rather un-English, his complexion being a rich olive, his rank hair dark and rather clammy—made still clammier by secret ointments, which, when he came fresh to a party, caused him to smell like 'boys'-love' (southern wood) steeped in lamp-oil. On occasion he wore curls—a double row—running almost horizontally around his head. But as these were sometimes noticeably absent, it was concluded that they were not altogether of Nature's making. By girls whose love for him had turned to hatred he had been nicknamed 'Mop', from this abundance of hair, which was long enough to rest upon his shoulders; as time passed the name more and more prevailed.

His fiddling possibly had the most to do with the fascination he exercised, for, to speak fairly, it could claim for itself a most peculiar and personal quality, like that in a moving preacher. There were tones in it which bred the immediate conviction that indolence and averseness to systematic application were all that lay between 'Mop' and the career of a second Paganini.

While playing he invariably closed his eyes; using no notes, and, as it were, allowing the violin to wander on at will into the most plaintive passages ever heard by rustic man. There was a certain lingual character in the supplicatory expressions he produced, which would well-nigh have drawn an ache from the heart of a gatepost. He could make any child in the parish, who was at all sensitive to music, burst into tears in a few minutes by simply fiddling one of the old dance-tunes he almost entirely affected—country jigs, reels, and 'Favourite Quick Steps' of the last century—some mutilated remains of which even now reappear as nameless phantoms in new quadrilles and gallops, where they are recognized only by the curious, or by such old-fashioned and far-between people as have been thrown with men like Wat Ollamoor in their early life.

His date was a little later than that of the old Mellstock quire-band which comprised the Dewys, Mail, and the rest—in fact, he did not rise above the horizon thereabout till those well-known musicians were disbanded as ecclesiastical functionaries. In their honest love of thoroughness they despised the new man's style. Theophilus Dewy (Reuben the tranter's younger brother) used to say there was no 'plumness' in it—no bowing, no solidity—it was all fantastical. And probably this was true. Anyhow, Mop had, very obviously, never bowed a note of church-music from his birth; he never once sat in the gallery of Mellstock church where the others had tuned their venerable psalmody so many hundreds of times; had never, in all likelihood, entered a church at all. All were devil's tunes in his repertory. 'He could no more play the Wold Hundredth to his true time than he could play the brazen serpent,' the tranter would say. (The brazen serpent was supposed in Mellstock to be a musical instrument particularly hard to blow.)

Occasionally Mop could produce the aforesaid moving effect upon the souls of grown-up persons, especially young women of fragile and responsive organization. Such an one was Car'line Aspent. Though she was already engaged to be married before she met him, Car'line, of them all, was the most influenced by Mop Ollamoor's heart-stealing melodies, to her discomfort, nay, positive pain and ultimate injury. She was a pretty, invocating, weak-mouthed girl, whose chief defect as a companion with her sex was a tendency to peevishness now and then. At this time she was not a resident in Mellstock parish where Mop lodged, but lived some miles off at Stickleford, further down the river.

How and where she first made acquaintance with him and his fiddling is not truly known, but the story was that it either began or was developed on one spring evening, when, in passing through Lower Mellstock, she chanced to pause on the bridge near his house to rest herself, and languidly leaned over the parapet. Mop was standing on his doorstep, as was his custom, spinning the insidious thread of semi- and demi-semiquavers from the E string of his fiddle for the benefit of passers-by, and laughing as the tears rolled down the cheeks of the little children hanging around him. Car'line pretended to be engrossed with the rippling of the stream under the arches, but in reality she was listening, as he knew. Presently the aching of the heart seized her simultaneously with a wild desire to glide airily in the mazes of an infinite dance. To shake off the fascination she resolved to go on, although it would be necessary to pass him as he played. On stealthily glancing ahead at the performer, she found to her relief that his eyes were closed in abandonment to instrumentation, and she strode on boldly. But when closer her step grew timid, her head convulsed itself more and more accordantly with the time of the melody, till she very nearly danced along. Gaining another glance at him when immediately opposite, she saw that *one* of his eyes was open, quizzing her as he smiled at her emotional state. Her gait could not divest itself of its compelled capers till she had gone a long way past the house; and Car'line was unable to shake off the strange infatuation for hours.

After that day, whenever there was to be in the neighbourhood a dance to which she could get an invitation, and where Mop Ollamoor was to be the musician, Car'line contrived to be present, though it sometimes involved a walk of several miles; for he did not play so often in Stickleford as elsewhere.

The next evidences of his influence over her were singular enough, and it would require a neurologist to fully explain them. She would be sitting quietly, any evening after dark, in the house of her father, the parish clerk, which stood in the middle of Stickleford village street, this being the high road between Lower Mellstock and Moreford, five miles eastward. Here, without a moment's warning, and in the midst of a general conversation between her father, sister, and the young man before alluded to, who devotedly wooed her in ignorance of her infatuation, she would start from her seat in the chimney-corner as if she had received a galvanic shock, and spring convulsively toward the ceiling; then she would burst into tears, and it was not till some half-hour had passed that she grew calm as usual. Her father, knowing her hysterical tendencies, was always excessively anxious about this trait in his youngest girl, and feared the attack to be a species of epileptic fit. Not so her sister Julia. Julia had found out what was the cause. At the moment before the jumping, only an exceptionally sensitive ear situated in the chimney-nook could have caught down the flue the beat of a man's footstep along the highway without. But it was in that footfall, for which she had been waiting, that the origin of Car'line's involuntary springing lay. The pedestrian was Mop Ollamoor, as the girl well knew; but his business that way was not to visit her; he sought another woman whom he spoke of as his Intended, and who lived at Moreford, two miles further on. On one, and only one, occasion did it happen that Car'line could not control her utterance; it was when her sister alone chanced to be present. 'Oh—oh—oh—!' she cried. 'He's going to *her*, and not coming to *me*!'

To do the fiddler justice he had not at first thought greatly of, or spoken much to, this girl of impressionable mould. But he had soon found out her secret, and could not resist a little byplay with her too easily hurt heart, as an interlude between his more serious love makings at Moreford. The two became well acquainted, though only by stealth, hardly a soul in Stickleford except her sister, and her lover Ned Hipcroft, being aware of the attachment. Her father disapproved of her coldness to Ned; her sister, too, hoped she might get over this nervous passion for a man of whom so little was known. The ultimate result was that Car'line's manly and simple wooer Edward found his suit becoming practically hopeless. He was a respectable mechanic, in a far sounder position than Mop the nominal horse-doctor; but when, before leaving her, Ned put his flat and final question, would she marry him, then and there, now or never, it was with little expectation of obtaining more than the negative she gave him. Though her father supported him and her sister supported him, he could not play the fiddle so as to draw your soul out of your body like a spider's thread, as Mop did, till you felt as limp as withy-wind and yearned for something to cling to. Indeed, Hipcroft had not the slightest ear for music; could not sing two notes in tune, much less play them.

The No he had expected and got from her, in spite of a preliminary encouragement, gave Ned a new start in life. It had been uttered in such a tone of sad entreaty that he resolved to persecute her no more; she should not even be distressed by a sight of his form in the distant perspective of the street and lane. He left the place, and his natural course was to London.

The railway to South Wessex was in process of construction,

but it was not as yet opened for traffic; and Hipcroft reached the capital by a six days' trudge on foot, as many a better man had done before him. He was one of the last of the artisan class who used that now extinct method of travel to the great centres of labour, so customary then from time immemorial.

In London he lived and worked regularly at his trade. More fortunate than many, his disinterested willingness recommended him from the first. During the ensuing four years he was never out of employment. He neither advanced nor receded in the modern sense; he improved as a workman, but he did not shift one jot in social position. About his love for Car'line he maintained a rigid silence. No doubt he often thought of her; but being always occupied, and having no relations at Stickleford, he held no communication with that part of the country, and showed no desire to return. In his quiet lodging in Lambeth he moved about after working-hours with the facility of a woman, doing his own cooking, attending to his stocking-heels, and shaping himself by degrees to a lifelong bachelorhood. For this conduct one is bound to advance the canonical reason that time could not efface from his heart the image of little Car'line Aspent—and it may be in part true; but there was also the inference that his was a nature not greatly dependent upon the ministrations of the other sex for its comforts.

The fourth year of his residence as a mechanic in London was the year of the Hyde Park Exhibition already mentioned, and at the construction of this huge glasshouse, then unexampled in the world's history, he worked daily. It was an era of great hope and activity among the nations and industries. Though Hipcroft was, in his small way, a central man in the movement, he plodded on with his usual outward placidity. Yet for him, too, the year was destined to have its surprises, for when the bustle of getting the building ready for the opening day was past, the ceremonies had been witnessed, and people were flocking thither from all parts of the globe, he received a letter from Car'line. Till that day the silence of four years between himself and Stickleford had never been broken.

She informed her old lover, in an uncertain penmanship, which suggested a trembling hand, of the trouble she had been put to in ascertaining his address, and then broached the subject which had prompted her to write. Four years ago, she said with the greatest delicacy of which she was capable, she had been so foolish as to refuse him. Her wilful wrong-headedness had since been a grief to her many times, and of late particularly. As for Mr Ollamoor, he had been absent almost as long as Ned—she did not know where. She would gladly marry Ned now if he were to ask her again, and be a tender little wife to him till her life's end.

A tide of warm feeling must have surged through Ned Hipcroft's frame on receipt of this news, if we may judge by the issue. Unquestionably he loved her still, even if not to the exclusion of every other happiness. This from his Car'line, she who had been dead to him these many years, alive to him again as of old, was in itself a pleasant, gratifying thing. Ned had grown so resigned to, or satisfied with, his lonely lot, that he probably would not have shown much jubilation at anything. Still, a certain ardour of preoccupation, after his first surprise, revealed how deeply her confession of faith in him had stirred him. Measured and methodical in his ways, he did not answer the letter that day, nor the next, nor the next. He was having 'a good think'. When he did answer it, there was a great deal of sound reasoning mixed in with the unmistakable tenderness of his reply; but the tenderness itself was sufficient to reveal that he was pleased with her straightforward frankness; that the anchorage she had once obtained in his heart was renewable, if it had not been continuously firm.

He told her—and as he wrote his lips twitched humorously

over the few gentle words of raillery he indited among the rest of his sentences—that it was all very well for her to come round at this time of day. Why wouldn't she have him when he wanted her? She had no doubt learned that he was not married, but suppose his affections had since been fixed on another? She ought to beg his pardon. Still, he was not the man to forget her. But considering how he had been used, and what he had suffered, she could not quite expect him to go down to Stickleford and fetch her. But if she would come to him, and say she was sorry, as was only fair; why, yes, he would marry her, knowing what a good little woman she was at the core. He added that the request for her to come to him was a less one to make than it would have been when he first left Stickleford, or even a few months ago; for the new railway into South Wessex was now open, and there had just begun to be run wonderfully contrived special trains, called excursion-trains, on account of the Great Exhibition; so that she could come up easily alone.

She said in her reply how good it was of him to treat her so generously, after her hot and cold treatment of him; that though she felt frightened at the magnitude of the journey, and was never as yet in a railway-train, having only seen one pass at a distance, she embraced his offer with all her heart; and would, indeed, own to him how sorry she was, and beg his pardon, and try to be a good wife always, and make up for lost time.

The remaining details of when and where were soon settled, Car'line informing him, for her ready identification in the crowd, that she would be wearing 'my new sprigged-laylock cotton gown', and Ned gaily responding that, having married her the morning after her arrival, he would make a day of it by taking her to the Exhibition. One early summer afternoon, accordingly, he came from his place of work, and hastened toward Waterloo Station to meet her. It was as wet and chilly as an English June day can occasionally be, but as he waited on the platform in the drizzle he glowed inwardly, and seemed to have something to live for again.

The 'excursion-train'—an absolutely new departure in the history of travel—was still a novelty on the Wessex line, and probably everywhere. Crowds of people had flocked to all the stations on the way up to witness the unwonted sight of so long a train's passage, even where they did not take advantage of the opportunity it offered. The seats for the humbler class of travellers in these early experiments in steam-locomotion, were open trucks, without any protection whatever from the wind and rain; and damp weather having set in with the afternoon, the unfortunate occupants of these vehicles were, on the train drawing up at the London terminus, found to be in a pitiable condition from their long journey; blue-faced, stiff-necked, sneezing, rain-beaten, chilled to the marrow, many of the men being hatless; in fact, they resembled people who had been out all night in an open boat on a rough sea, rather than inland excursionists for pleasure. The women had in some degree protected themselves by turning up the skirts of their gowns over their heads, but as by this arrangement they were additionally exposed about the hips, they were all more or less in a sorry plight.

In the bustle and crush of alighting forms of both sexes which followed the entry of the huge concatenation into the station, Ned Hipcroft soon discerned the slim little figure his eye was in search of, in the sprigged lilac, as described. She came up to him with a frightened smile—still pretty, though so damp, weather-beaten, and shivering from long exposure to the wind.

'O, Ned!' she sputtered, 'I—I—' He clasped her in his arms and kissed her, whereupon she burst into a flood of tears.

'You are wet, my poor dear! I hope you'll not get cold,' he said. And surveying her and her multifarious surrounding packages, he noticed that by the hand she led a toddling child—a little girl of three or so—whose hood was as clammy and tender face as blue as those of the other travellers.

'Who is this—somebody you know?' asked Ned curiously.

'Yes, Ned. She's mine.'

'Yours?'

'Yes—my own.'

'Your own child?'

'Yes!'

'Well—as God's in—'

'Ned, I didn't name it in my letter, because, you see, it would have been so hard to explain! I thought that when we met I could tell you how she happened to be born, so much better than in writing! I hope you'll excuse it this once, dear Ned, and scold me, now I've come so many, many miles!'

'This means Mr Mop Ollamoor, I reckon!' said Hipcroft, gazing palely at them from the distance of the yard or two to which he had withdrawn with a start.

Car'line gasped. 'But he's been gone away for years!' she supplicated. 'And I never had a young man before! And I was so onlucky to be catched the first time, though some of the girls down there go on like anything!'

Ned remained in silence, pondering.

'You'll forgive me, dear Ned?' she added, beginning to sob outright. 'I haven't taken 'ee in after all, because—because you can pack us back again, if you want to; though 'tis hundreds o' miles, and so wet, and night a-coming on, and I with no money!'

'What the devil can I do!' Hipcroft groaned.

A more pitiable picture than the pair of helpless creatures presented was never seen on a rainy day, as they stood on the great, gaunt, puddled platform, a whiff of drizzle blowing under the roof upon them now and then; the pretty attire in which they had started from Stickleford in the early morning bemuddled and sodden, weariness on their faces, and fear of him in their eyes; for the child began to look as if she thought she too had done some wrong, remaining in an appalled silence till the tears rolled down her chubby cheeks.

'What's the matter, my little maid?' said Ned mechanically.

'I do want to go home!' she let out, in tones that told of a bursting heart. 'And my totties be cold, an' I shan't have no bread an' butter no more!'

'I don't know what to say to it all!' declared Ned, his own eye moist as he turned and walked a few steps with his head down; then regarded them again point-blank. From the child escaped troubled breaths and silently welling tears.

'Want some bread and butter, do 'ee?' he said, with factitious hardness.

'Ye-e-s!'

'Well, I daresay I can get 'ee a bit! Naturally, you must want some. And you, too, for that matter, Car'line.'

'I do feel a little hungered. But I can keep it off,' she murmured.

'Folk shouldn't do that,' he said gruffly... 'There, come along!' He caught up the child, as he added, 'You must bide here tonight, anyhow, I s'pose! What can you do otherwise? I'll get 'ee some tea and victuals; and as for this job, I'm sure I don't know what to say! This is the way out.'

They pursued their way, without speaking, to Ned's lodgings, which were not far off. There he dried them and made them comfortable, and prepared tea; they thankfully sat down. The ready-made household of which he suddenly found himself the head imparted a cosy aspect to his room, and a paternal one to himself. Presently he turned to the child and kissed her now blooming cheeks; and, looking wistfully at Car'line, kissed her also.

'I don't see how I can send you back all them miles,' he

growled, 'now you've come all the way o' purpose to join me. But you must trust me, Car'line, and show you've real faith in me. Well, do you feel better now, my little woman?'

The child nodded, her mouth being otherwise occupied.

'I did trust you, Ned, in coming; and I shall always!'

Thus, without any definite agreement to forgive her, he tacitly acquiesced in the fate that Heaven had sent him; and on the day of their marriage (which was not quite so soon as he had expected it could be, on account of the time necessary for banns) he took her to the Exhibition when they came back from church, as he had promised. While standing near a large mirror in one of the courts devoted to furniture, Car'line started, for in the glass appeared the reflection of a form exactly resembling Mop Ollamoor's—so exactly, that it seemed impossible to believe anybody but that artist in person to be the original. On passing round the objects which hemmed in Ned, her, and the child from a direct view, no Mop was to be seen. Whether he were really in London or not at that time was never known; and Car'line always stoutly denied that her readiness to go and meet Ned in town arose from any rumour that Mop had also gone thither; which denial there was no reasonable ground for doubting.

And then the year glided away, and the Exhibition folded itself up and became a thing of the past. The park trees that had been enclosed for six months were again exposed to the winds and storms, and the sod grew green anew. Ned found that Car'line resolved herself into a very good wife and companion, though she had made herself what is called cheap to him; but in that she was like another domestic article, a cheap teapot, which often brews better tea than a dear one.

One autumn Hipcroft found himself with but little work to do, and a prospect of less for the winter. Both being country born and bred, they fancied they would like to live again in their natural atmosphere. It was accordingly decided between them that they should leave the pent-up London lodging, and that Ned should seek out employment near his native place, his wife and her daughter staying with Car'line's father during the search for occupation and an abode of their own.

Tinglings of pride pervaded Car'line's spasmodic little frame as she journeyed down with Ned to the place she had left two or three years before, in silence and under a cloud. To return to where she had once been despised, a smiling London wife with a distinct London accent, was a triumph which the world did not witness every day.

The train did not stop at the petty roadside station that lay nearest to Stickleford, and the trio went on to Casterbridge. Ned thought it a good opportunity to make a few preliminary inquiries for employment at workshops in the borough where he had been known; and feeling cold from her journey, and it being dry underfoot and only dusk as yet, with a moon on the point of rising, Car'line and her little girl walked on toward Stickleford, leaving Ned to follow at a quicker pace, and pick her up at a certain halfway house, widely known as an inn.

The woman and child pursued the well-remembered way comfortably enough, though they were both becoming wearied. In the course of three miles they had passed Heedless-William's Pond, the familiar landmark by Bloom's End, and were drawing near the Quiet Woman Inn, a lone roadside hostel on the lower verge of the Egdon Heath, since and for many years abolished. In stepping up toward it Car'line heard more voices within than had formerly been customary at such an hour, and she learned that an auction of fat stock had been held near the spot that afternoon. The child would be the better for a rest as well as herself, she thought, and she entered.

The guests and customers overflowed into the passage, and Car'line had no sooner crossed the threshold than a man whom she remembered by sight came forward with a glass and mug in his hands towards a friend leaning against the wall; but, seeing her, very gallantly offered her a drink of the liquor, which was gin-and-beer hot, pouring her out a tumblerful and saying, in a moment or two: 'Surely, 'tis little Car'line Aspent that was down at Stickleford?'

She assented, and, though she did not exactly want this beverage, she drank it since it was offered, and her entertainer begged her to come in further and sit down. Once within the room she found that all the persons present were seated close against the walls, and there being a chair vacant she did the same. An explanation of their position occurred the next moment. In the opposite corner stood Mop, rosining his bow and looking just the same as ever. The company had cleared the middle of the room for dancing, and they were about to dance again. As she wore a veil to keep off the wind she did not think he had recognized her, or could possibly guess the identity of the child; and to her satisfied surprise she found that she could confront him quite calmly—mistress of herself in the dignity her London life had given her. Before she had quite emptied her glass the dance was called, the dancers formed in two lines, the music sounded, and the figure began.

Then matters changed for Car'line. A tremor quickened itself to life in her, and her hand so shook that she could hardly set down her glass. It was not the dance nor the dancers, but the notes of that old violin which thrilled the London wife, these having still all the witchery that she had so well known of yore, and under which she had used to lose her power of independent will. How it all came back! There was the fiddling figure against the wall; the large, oily, mop-like head of him, and beneath the mop the face with closed eyes.

After the first moments of paralyzed reverie the familiar tune in the familiar rendering made her laugh and shed tears simultaneously. Then a man at the bottom of the dance, whose partner had dropped away, stretched out his hand and beckoned to her to take the place. She did not want to dance; she entreated by signs to be left where she was, but she was entreating of the tune and its player rather than of the dancing man. The saltatory tendency which the fiddler and his cunning instrument had ever been able to start in her was seizing Car'line just as it had done in earlier years, possibly assisted by the gin-and-beer hot. Tired as she was she grasped her little girl by the hand, and plunging in at the bottom of the figure, whirled about with the rest. She found that her companions were mostly people of the neighbouring hamlets and farms—Bloom's End, Mellstock, Lewgate, and elsewhere; and by degrees she was recognized as she convulsively danced on, wishing that Mop would cease and let her heart rest from the aching he caused, and her feet also.

After long and many minutes the dance ended, when she was urged to fortify herself with more gin-and-beer; which she did, feeling very weak and overpowered with hysteric emotion. She refrained from unveiling, to keep Mop in ignorance of her presence, if possible. Several of the guests having left, Car'line hastily wiped her lips and also turned to go; but, according to the account of some who remained, at that very moment a five-handed reel was proposed, in which two or three begged her to join.

She declined on the plea of being tired and having to walk to Stickleford, when Mop began aggressively tweedling 'My Fancy-Lad', in D major, as the air to which the reel was to be footed. He must have recognized her, though she did not know it, for it was the strain of all seductive strains which she was least able to resist—the one he had played when she was leaning over the bridge at the date of their first acquaintance. Car'line stepped despairingly into the middle of the room with the other four.

Reels were resorted to hereabouts at this time by the more robust spirits, for the reduction of superfluous energy which the ordinary figure-dances were not powerful enough to exhaust. As everybody knows, or does not know, the five reelers stood in the form of a cross, the reel being performed by each line of three alternately, the persons who successively came to the middle place dancing in both directions. Car'line soon found herself in this place, the axis of the whole performance, and could not get out of it, the tune turning into the first part without giving her opportunity. And now she began to suspect that Mop did know her, and was doing this on purpose, though whenever she stole a glance at him his closed eyes betokened obliviousness to everything outside his own brain. She continued to wend her way through the figure of eight that was formed by her course, the fiddler introducing into his notes the wild and agonizing sweetness of a living voice in one too highly wrought; its pathos running high and running low in endless variation, projecting through her nerves excruciating spasms, a sort of blissful torture. The room swam, the tune was endless; and in about a quarter of an hour the only other woman in the figure dropped out exhausted, and sank panting on a bench.

The reel instantly resolved itself into a four-handed one. Car'line would have given anything to leave off; but she had, or fancied she had, no power, while Mop played such tunes; and thus another ten minutes slipped by, a haze of dust now clouding the candles, the floor being of stone, sanded. Then another dancer fell out—one of the men—and went into the passage in a frantic search for liquor. To turn the figure into a three-handed reel was the work of a second, Mop modulating at the same time into 'The Fairy Dance', as better suited to the contracted movement, and no less one of those foods of love which, as manufactured by his bow, had always intoxicated her.

In a reel for three there was no rest whatever, and four or

five minutes were enough to make her remaining two partners, now thoroughly blown, stamp their last bar, and, like their predecessors, limp off into the next room to get something to drink. Car'line, half-stifled inside her veil, was left dancing alone, the apartment now being empty of everybody save herself, Mop, and their little girl.

She flung up the veil, and cast her eyes upon him, as if imploring him to withdraw himself and his acoustic magnetism from the atmosphere. Mop opened one of his own orbs, as though for the first time, fixed it peeringly upon her, and smiling dreamily, threw into his strains the reserve of expression which he could not afford to waste on a big and noisy dance. Crowds of little chromatic subtleties, capable of drawing tears from a statue, proceeded straightway from the ancient fiddle, as if it were dying of the emotion which had been pent up within it ever since its banishment from some Italian city where it first took shape and sound. There was that in the look of Mop's one dark eye which said: 'You cannot leave off, dear, whether you would or no!' and it bred in her a paroxysm of desperation that defied him to tire her down.

She thus continued to dance alone, defiantly as she thought, but in truth slavishly and abjectly, subject to every wave of the melody, and probed by the gimlet-like gaze of her fascinator's open eye; keeping up at the same time a feeble smile in his face, as feint to signify it was still her own pleasure which led her on. A terrified embarrassment as to what she could say to him if she were to leave off, had its unrecognized share in keeping her going. The child, who was beginning to be distressed by the strange situation, came up and whimpered: 'Stop, mother, stop, and let's go home!' as she seized Car'line's hand.

Suddenly Car'line sank staggering to the floor, and rolling over on her face, prone she remained. Mop's fiddle thereupon emitted an elfin shriek of finality; stepping quickly down from the nine-gallon beer-cask which had formed his rostrum, he went to the little girl, who disconsolately bent over her mother.

The guests who had gone into the back room for liquor and change of air, hearing something unusual, trooped back hitherward, where they endeavoured to revive poor, weak Car'line by blowing her with the bellows and opening the window. Ned, her husband, who had been detained in Casterbridge, as aforesaid, came along the road at this juncture, and hearing excited voices through the open casement, and to his great surprise, the mention of his wife's name, he entered amid the rest upon the scene. Car'line was now in convulsions, weeping violently, and for a long time nothing could be done with her. While he was sending for a cart to take her onward to Stickleford Hipcroft anxiously inquired how it had all happened; and then the assembly explained that a fiddler formerly known in the locality had lately visited his old haunts, and had taken upon himself without invitation to play that evening at the inn. Ned demanded the fiddler's name, and they said Ollamoor.

'Ah!' exclaimed Ned, looking round him. 'Where is he, and where—where's my little girl?'

Ollamoor had disappeared, and so had the child. Hipcroft was in ordinary a quiet and tractable fellow, but a determination which was to be feared settled in his face now. 'Blast him!' he cried. 'I'll beat his skull in for'n, if I swing for it tomorrow!'

He had rushed to the poker which lay on the hearth, and hastened down the passage, the people following. Outside the house, on the other side of the highway, a mass of dark heathland rose sullenly upward to its not easily accessible interior, a ravined plateau, whereon jutted into the sky, at the distance of a couple of miles, the fir-woods of Mistover backed by the Yalbury coppices—a place of Dantesque gloom at this hour, which would have afforded secure hiding for a battery of artillery, much less a man and a child.

Some other men plunged thitherward with him, and more went along the road. They were gone about twenty minutes altogether, returning without result to the inn. Ned sat down in the settle, and clasped his forehead with his hands.

'Well—what a fool the man is, and hev been all these years, if he thinks the child his, as a' do seem to!' they whispered. 'And everybody else knowing otherwise!'

'No, I don't think 'tis mine!' cried Ned hoarsely, as he looked up from his hands. 'But she is mine, all the same! Ha'n't I nussed her? Ha'n't I fed her and teached her? Ha'n't I played wi' her? O, little Carry—gone with that rogue—gone!'

'You ha'n't lost your mis'ess, anyhow,' they said to console him. 'She's throwed up the sperrits, and she is feeling better, and she's more to 'ee than a child that isn't yours.'

'She isn't! She's not so particular much to me, especially now she's lost the little maid! But Carry's everything!'

'Well, ver' like you'll find her tomorrow.'

'Ah—but shall I? Yet he *can't* hurt her—surely he can't! Well—how's Car'line now? I am ready. Is the cart here?'

She was lifted into the vehicle, and they sadly lumbered on toward Stickleford. Next day she was calmer; but the fits were still upon her; and her will seemed shattered. For the child she appeared to show singularly little anxiety, though Ned was nearly distracted. It was nevertheless quite expected that the impish Mop would restore the lost one after a freak of a day or two; but time went on, and neither he nor she could be heard of, and Hipcroft murmured that perhaps he was exercising upon her some unholy musical charm, as he had done upon Car'line herself. Weeks passed, and still they could obtain no clue either to the fiddler's whereabouts or to the girl's; and how he could have induced her to go with him remained a mystery.

Then Ned, who had obtained only temporary employment in the neighbourhood, took a sudden hatred toward his native district, and a rumour reaching his ears through the police that a somewhat similar man and child had been seen at a fair near London, he playing a violin, she dancing on stilts, a new interest in the capital took possession of Hipcroft with an intensity which would scarcely allow him time to pack before returning thither.

He did not, however, find the lost one, though he made it the entire business of his over-hours to stand about in by-streets in the hope of discovering her, and would start up in the night, saying, 'That rascal's torturing her to maintain him!' To which his wife would answer peevishly, 'Don't 'ee raft yourself so, Ned! You prevent my getting a bit o' rest! He won't hurt her!' and fall asleep again.

That Carry and her father had emigrated to America was the general opinion; Mop, no doubt, finding the girl a highly desirable companion when he had trained her to keep him by her earnings as a dancer. There, for that matter, they may be performing in some capacity now, though he must be an old scamp verging on three-score-and-ten, and she a woman of four-and-forty.

6

THE SON'S VETO

I

To the eyes of a man viewing it from behind, the nut-brown hair was a wonder and a mystery. Under the black beaver hat, surmounted by its tuft of black feathers, the long locks, braided and twisted and coiled like the rushes of a basket, composed a rare, if somewhat barbaric, example of ingenious art. One could understand such weavings and coilings being wrought to last intact for a year, or even a calendar month; but that they should be all demolished regularly at bedtime, after a single day of permanence, seemed a reckless waste of successful fabrication.

And she had done it all herself, poor thing. She had no maid, and it was almost the only accomplishment she could boast of. Hence the unstinted pains.

She was a young invalid lady—not so very much of an invalid—sitting in a wheeled chair, which had been pulled up in the front part of a green enclosure, close to a bandstand, where a concert was going on, during a warm June afternoon. It had place in one of the minor parks or private gardens that are to be found in the suburbs of London, and was the effort of a local association to raise money for some charity. There are worlds within worlds in the great city, and though nobody outside the immediate district had ever heard of the charity, or the band, or the garden, the enclosure was filled with an interested audience sufficiently informed on all these.

As the strains proceeded many of the listeners observed the chaired lady, whose back hair, by reason of her prominent position, so challenged inspection. Her face was not easily discernible, but the aforesaid cunning tress-weavings, the white ear and poll, and the curve of a cheek which was neither flaccid nor sallow, were signals that led to the expectation of good beauty in front. Such expectations are not infrequently disappointed as soon as the disclosure comes; and in the present case, when the lady, by a turn of the head, at length revealed herself, she was not so handsome as the people behind her had supposed, and even hoped—they did not know why.

For one thing (alas! the commonness of this complaint), she was less young than they had fancied her to be. Yet attractive her face unquestionably was, and not at all sickly. The revelation of its details came each time she turned to talk to a boy of twelve or thirteen who stood beside her, and the shape of whose hat and jacket implied that he belonged to a well-known public school. The immediate bystanders could hear that he called her 'Mother.'

When the end of the recital was reached, and the audience withdrew, many chose to find their way out by passing at her elbow. Almost all turned their heads to take a full and near look at the interesting woman, who remained stationary in the chair till the way should be clear enough for her to be wheeled out without obstruction. As if she expected their glances, and did not mind gratifying their curiosity, she met the eyes of several of her observers by lifting her own, showing these to be soft, brown, and affectionate orbs, a little plaintive in their regard.

She was conducted out of the gardens, and passed along

the pavement till she disappeared from view, the schoolboy walking beside her. To inquiries made by some persons who watched her away, the answer came that she was the second wife of the incumbent of a neighbouring parish, and that she was lame. She was generally believed to be a woman with a story—an innocent one, but a story of some sort or other.

In conversing with her on their way home the boy who walked at her elbow said that he hoped his father had not missed them.

'He have been so comfortable these last few hours that I am sure he cannot have missed us,' she replied.

'*Has*, dear mother—not *have*!' exclaimed the public-school boy, with an impatient fastidiousness that was almost harsh. 'Surely you know that by this time!'

His mother hastily adopted the correction, and did not resent his making it, or retaliate, as she might well have done, by bidding him to wipe that crumby mouth of his, whose condition had been caused by surreptitious attempts to eat a piece of cake without taking it out of the pocket wherein it lay concealed. After this the pretty woman and the boy went onward in silence.

That question of grammar bore upon her history, and she fell into reverie, of a somewhat sad kind to all appearance. It might have been assumed that she was wondering if she had done wisely in shaping her life as she had shaped it, to bring out such a result as this.

In a remote nook in North Wessex, forty miles from London, near the thriving county-town of Aldbrickham, there stood a pretty village with its church and parsonage, which she knew well enough, but her son had never seen. It was her native village, Gaymead, and the first event bearing upon her present situation had occurred at that place when she was only a girl of nineteen.

How well she remembered it, that first act in her little tragi-comedy, the death of her reverend husband's first wife. It happened on a spring evening, and she who now and for many years had filled that first wife's place was then parlourmaid in the parson's house.

When everything had been done that could be done, and the death was announced, she had gone out in the dusk to visit her parents, who were living in the same village, to tell them the sad news. As she opened the white swing-gate and looked towards the trees which rose westward, shutting out the pale light of the evening sky, she discerned, without much surprise, the figure of a man standing in the hedge, though she roguishly exclaimed as a matter of form, 'Oh, Sam, how you frightened me!'

He was a young gardener of her acquaintance. She told him the particulars of the late event, and they stood silent, these two young people, in that elevated, calmly philosophic mind which is engendered when a tragedy has happened close at hand, and has not happened to the philosophers themselves. But it had its bearing upon their relations.

'And will you stay on now at the Vicarage, just the same?' asked he.

She had hardly thought of that. 'Oh, yes—I suppose!' she said. 'Everything will be just as usual, I imagine?'

He walked beside her towards her mother's. Presently his arm stole round her waist. She gently removed it; but he placed it there again, and she yielded the point. 'You see, dear Sophy, you don't know that you'll stay on; you may want a home; and I shall be ready to offer one some day, though I may not be ready just yet.

'Why, Sam, how can you be so fast! I've never even said I liked 'ee; and it is all your own doing, coming after me!'

'Still, it is nonsense to say I am not to have a try at you

like the rest.' He stooped to kiss her a farewell, for they had reached her mother's door.

'No, Sam; you sha'n't!' she cried, putting her hand over his mouth. 'You ought to be more serious on such a night as this.' And she bade him adieu without allowing him to kiss her or to come indoors.

The vicar just left a widower was at this time a man about forty years of age, of good family, and childless. He had led a secluded existence in this college living, partly because there were no resident landowners; and his loss now intensified his habit of withdrawal from outward observation. He was still less seen than heretofore, kept himself still less in time with the rhythm and racket of the movements called progress in the world without. For many months after his wife's decease the economy of his household remained as before; the cook, the housemaid, the parlourmaid, and the man out-of-doors performed their duties or left them undone, just as Nature prompted them—the vicar knew not which. It was then represented to him that his servants seemed to have nothing to do in his small family of one. He was struck with the truth of this representation, and decided to cut down his establishment. But he was forestalled by Sophy, the parlourmaid, who said one evening that she wished to leave him.

'And why?' said the parson.

'Sam Hobson has asked me to marry him, sir.'

'Well—do you want to marry?'

'Not much. But it would be a home for me. And we have heard that one of us will have to leave.'

A day or two after she said: 'I don't want to leave just yet, sir, if you don't wish it. Sam and I have quarrelled.'

He looked up at her. He had hardly ever observed her before, though he had been frequently conscious of her soft presence in the room. What a kitten-like, flexuous, tender creature she was! She was the only one of the servants with whom he came into immediate and continuous relation. What should he do if Sophy were gone?

Sophy did not go, but one of the others did, and things went on quietly again.

When Mr Twycott, the vicar, was ill, Sophy brought up his meals to him, and she had no sooner left the room one day than he heard a noise on the stairs. She had slipped down with the tray, and so twisted her foot that she could not stand. The village surgeon was called in; the vicar got better, but Sophy was incapacitated for a long time; and she was informed that she must never again walk much or engage in any occupation which required her to stand long on her feet. As soon as she was comparatively well she spoke to him alone. Since she was forbidden to walk and bustle about, and, indeed, could not do so, it became her duty to leave. She could very well work at something sitting down, and she had an aunt a seamstress.

The parson had been very greatly moved by what she had suffered on his account, and he exclaimed, 'No, Sophy; lame or not lame, I cannot let you go. You must never leave me again!'

He came close to her, and, though she could never exactly tell how it happened, she became conscious of his lips upon her cheek. He then asked her to marry him. Sophy did not exactly love him, but she had a respect for him which almost amounted to veneration. Even if she had wished to get away from him she hardly dared refuse a personage so reverend and august in her eyes, and she assented forthwith to be his wife.

Thus it happened that one fine morning, when the doors of the church were naturally open for ventilation, and the singing birds fluttered in and alighted on the tie-beams of the roof, there was a marriage-service at the communion-rails, which hardly a soul knew of. The parson and a neighbouring curate had entered at one door, and Sophy at another, followed by two necessary persons, whereupon in a short time there emerged a newly-made husband and wife.

Mr Twycott knew perfectly well that he had committed social suicide by this step, despite Sophy's spotless character, and he had taken his measures accordingly. An exchange of livings had been arranged with an acquaintance who was incumbent of a church in the south of London, and as soon as possible the couple removed thither, abandoning their pretty country home, with trees and shrubs and glebe, for a narrow, dusty house in a long, straight street, and their fine peal of bells for the wretchedest one-tongued clangour that ever tortured mortal ears. It was all on her account. They were, however, away from every one who had known her former position; and also under less observation from without than they would have had to put up with in any country parish.

Sophy the woman was as charming a partner as a man could possess, though Sophy the lady had her deficiencies. She showed a natural aptitude for little domestic refinements, so far as related to things and manners; but in what is called culture she was less intuitive. She had now been married more than fourteen years, and her husband had taken much trouble with her education; but she still held confused ideas on the use of 'was' and 'were,' which did not beget a respect for her among the few acquaintances she made. Her great grief in this relation was that her only child, on whose education no expense had been and would be spared, was now old enough to perceive these deficiencies in his mother, and not only to see them but to feel irritated at their existence.

Thus she lived on in the city, and wasted hours in braiding her beautiful hair, till her once apple cheeks waned to pink of the very faintest. Her foot had never regained its natural strength after the accident, and she was mostly obliged to avoid walking altogether. Her husband had grown to like London for its freedom and its domestic privacy; but he was twenty years his Sophy's senior, and had latterly been seized with a serious illness. On this day, however, he had seemed to be well enough to justify her accompanying her son Randolph to the concert.

II

The next time we get a glimpse of her is when she appears in the mournful attire of a widow.

Mr Twycott had never rallied, and now lay in a well-packed cemetery to the south of the great city, where, if all the dead it contained had stood erect and alive, not one would have known him or recognized his name. The boy had dutifully followed him to the grave, and was now again at school.

Throughout these changes Sophy had been treated like the child she was in nature though not in years. She was left with no control over anything that had been her husband's beyond her modest personal income. In his anxiety lest her inexperience should be overreached he had safeguarded with trustees all he possibly could. The completion of the boy's course at the public school, to be followed in due time by Oxford and ordination, had been all previsioned and arranged, and she really had nothing to occupy her in the world but to eat and drink, and make a business of indolence, and go on weaving and coiling the nut-brown hair, merely keeping a home open for the son whenever he came to her during vacations.

Foreseeing his probable decease long years before her, her husband in his lifetime had purchased for her use a semi-detached villa in the same long, straight road whereon the church and parsonage faced, which was to be hers as long as she chose to live in it. Here she now resided, looking out upon the fragment of lawn in front, and through the railings at the ever-flowing traffic; or, bending forward over the windowsill on the first floor, stretching her eyes far up and down the vista of sooty trees, hazy air, and drab house-facades, along which echoed the noises common to a suburban main thoroughfare.

Somehow, her boy, with his aristocratic school-knowledge, his grammars, and his aversions, was losing those wide infantine sympathies, extending as far as to the sun and moon themselves, with which he, like other children, had been born, and which his mother, a child of nature herself, had loved in him; he was reducing their compass to a population of a few thousand wealthy and titled people, the mere veneer of a thousand million or so of others who did not interest him at all. He drifted further and further away from her. Sophy's milieu being a suburb of minor tradesmen and under-clerks, and her almost only companions the two servants of her own house, it was not surprising that after her husband's death she soon lost the little artificial tastes she had acquired from him, and became—in her son's eyes—a mother whose mistakes and origin it was his painful lot as a gentleman to blush for. As yet he was far from being man enough—if he ever would be—to rate these sins of hers at their true infinitesimal value beside the yearning fondness that welled up and remained penned in her heart till it should be more fully accepted by him, or by some other person or thing. If he had lived at home with her he would have had all of it; but he seemed to require so very little in present circumstances, and it remained stored.

Her life became insupportably dreary; she could not take walks, and had no interest in going for drives, or, indeed, in travelling anywhere. Nearly two years passed without an event, and still she looked on that suburban road, thinking of the village in which she had been born, and whither she would have gone back—O how gladly!—even to work in the fields.

Taking no exercise, she often could not sleep, and would rise in the night or early morning and look out upon the then vacant thoroughfare, where the lamps stood like sentinels waiting for some procession to go by. An approximation to such a procession was indeed made early every morning about one o'clock, when the country vehicles passed up with loads of vegetables for Covent Garden market. She often saw them creeping along at this silent and dusky hour—wagon after wagon, bearing green bastions of cabbages nodding to their fall, yet never falling, walls of baskets enclosing masses of beans and peas, pyramids of snow-white turnips, swaying howdahs of mixed produce—creeping along behind aged night-horses, who seemed ever patiently wondering between their hollow coughs why they had always to work at that still hour when all other sentient creatures were privileged to rest. Wrapped in a cloak, it was soothing to watch and sympathize with them when depression and nervousness hindered sleep, and to see how the fresh green-stuff brightened to life as it came opposite the lamp, and how the sweating animals steamed and shone with their miles of travel.

They had an interest, almost a charm, for Sophy, these semi-rural people and vehicles moving in an urban atmosphere, leading a life quite distinct from that of the daytime toilers on the same road. One morning a man who accompanied a wagon-load of potatoes gazed rather hard at the house-fronts as he passed, and with a curious emotion she thought his form was familiar to her. She looked out for him again. His being an old-fashioned conveyance, with a yellow front, it was easily recognizable, and on the third night after she saw it a second time. The man alongside was, as she had fancied, Sam Hobson, formerly gardener at Gaymead, who would at one time have married her.

She had occasionally thought of him, and wondered if life in a cottage with him would not have been a happier lot than the life she had accepted. She had not thought of him passionately, but her now dismal situation lent an interest to his resurrection—a tender interest which it is impossible to exaggerate. She went back to bed, and began thinking. When did these market-gardeners, who travelled up to town so regularly at one or two in the morning, come back? She dimly recollected seeing their empty wagons, hardly noticeable amid the ordinary day-traffic, passing down at some hour before noon.

It was only April, but that morning, after breakfast, she had the window opened, and sat looking out, the feeble sun shining full upon her. She affected to sew, but her eyes never left the street. Between ten and eleven the desired wagon, now unladen, reappeared on its return journey. But Sam was not looking round him then, and drove on in a reverie.

'Sam!' cried she.

Turning with a start, his face lighted up. He called to him a little boy to hold the horse, alighted, and came and stood under her window.

'I can't come down easily, Sam, or I would!' she said. 'Did you know I lived here?'

'Well, Mrs Twycott, I knew you lived along here somewhere. I have often looked out for 'ee.'

He briefly explained his own presence on the scene. He had long since given up his gardening in the village near Aldbrickham, and was now manager at a market-gardener's on the south side of London, it being part of his duty to go up to Covent Garden with wagon-loads of produce two or three times a week. In answer to her curious inquiry, he admitted that he had come to this particular district because he had seen in the Aldbrickham paper, a year or two before, the announcement of the death in South London of the aforetime vicar of Gaymead, which had revived an interest in her dwelling-place that he could not extinguish, leading him to hover about the locality till his present post had been secured.

They spoke of their native village in dear old North Wessex, the spots in which they had played together as children. She tried to feel that she was a dignified personage now, that she must not be too confidential with Sam. But she could not keep it up, and the tears hanging in her eyes were indicated in her voice.

'You are not happy, Mrs Twycott, I'm afraid?' he said.

'O, of course not! I lost my husband only the year before last.'

'Ah! I meant in another way. You'd like to be home again?'

'This is my home—for life. The house belongs to me. But I understand—' She let it out then. 'Yes, Sam. I long for home—*our* home! I *should* like to be there, and never leave it, and die there.' But she remembered herself. 'That's only a momentary feeling. I have a son, you know, a dear boy. He's at school now.'

'Somewhere handy, I suppose? I see there's lots on 'em along this road.'

'O no! Not in one of these wretched holes! At a public school—one of the most distinguished in England.'

'Chok' it all! Of course! I forget, ma'am, that you've been a lady for so many years.'

'No, I am not a lady,' she said sadly. 'I never shall be. But he's a gentleman, and that—makes it—O how difficult for me!'

III

The acquaintance thus oddly reopened proceeded apace. She often looked out to get a few words with him, by night or by day. Her sorrow was that she could not accompany her one old friend on foot a little way, and talk more freely than she could do while he paused before the house. One night, at the beginning of June, when she was again on the watch after an absence of some days from the window, he entered the gate and said softly, 'Now, wouldn't some air do you good? I've only half a load this morning. Why not ride up to Covent Garden with me? There's a nice seat on the cabbages, where I've spread a sack. You can be home again in a cab before anybody is up.'

She refused at first, and then, trembling with excitement, hastily finished her dressing, and wrapped herself up in cloak and veil, afterwards sidling downstairs by the aid of the handrail, in a way she could adopt on an emergency. When she had opened the door she found Sam on the step, and he lifted her bodily on his strong arm across the little forecourt into his vehicle. Not a soul was visible or audible in the infinite length of the straight, flat highway, with its ever-waiting lamps converging to points in each direction. The air was fresh as country air at this hour, and the stars shone, except to the northeastward, where there was a whitish light—the dawn. Sam carefully placed her in the seat, and drove on.

They talked as they had talked in old days, Sam pulling himself up now and then, when he thought himself too familiar. More than once she said with misgiving that she wondered if she ought to have indulged in the freak. 'But I am so lonely in my house,' she added, 'and this makes me so happy!'

'You must come again, dear Mrs Twycott. There is no time o' day for taking the air like this.'

It grew lighter and lighter. The sparrows became busy in the streets, and the city waxed denser around them. When they approached the river it was day, and on the bridge they beheld the full blaze of morning sunlight in the direction of St. Paul's, the river glistening towards it, and not a craft stirring.

Near Covent Garden he put her into a cab, and they parted, looking into each other's faces like the very old friends they were. She reached home without adventure, limped to the door, and let herself in with her latchkey unseen.

The air and Sam's presence had revived her: her cheeks were quite pink—almost beautiful. She had something to live for in addition to her son. A woman of pure instincts, she knew there had been nothing really wrong in the journey, but supposed it conventionally to be very wrong indeed.

Soon, however, she gave way to the temptation of going with him again, and on this occasion their conversation was distinctly tender, and Sam said he never should forget her, notwithstanding that she had served him rather badly at one time. After much hesitation he told her of a plan it was in his power to carry out, and one he should like to take in hand, since he did not care for London work: it was to set up as a master greengrocer down at Aldbrickham, the county-town of their native place. He knew of an opening—a shop kept by aged people who wished to retire.

'And why don't you do it, then, Sam?' she asked with a slight heart-sinking.

'Because I'm not sure if—you'd join me. I know you wouldn't—couldn't! Such a lady as ye've been so long, you couldn't be a wife to a man like me.'

'I hardly suppose I could!' she assented, also frightened at the idea.

'If you could,' he said eagerly, 'you'd on'y have to sit in the back parlour and look through the glass partition when I was away sometimes—just to keep an eye on things. The lameness wouldn't hinder that...I'd keep you as genteel as ever I could, dear Sophy—if I might think of it!' he pleaded.

'Sam, I'll be frank,' she said, putting her hand on his. 'If it were only myself I would do it, and gladly, though everything I possess would be lost to me by marrying again.'

'I don't mind that! It's more independent.'

'That's good of you, dear, dear Sam. But there's something else. I have a son...I almost fancy when I am miserable sometimes that he is not really mine, but one I hold in trust for my late husband. He seems to belong so little to me personally, so entirely to his dead father. He is so much educated and I so little that I do not feel dignified enough to be his mother... Well, he would have to be told.'

'Yes. Unquestionably.' Sam saw her thought and her fear. 'Still, you can do as you like, Sophy—Mrs Twycott,' he added. 'It is not you who are the child, but he.'

'Ah, you don't know! Sam, if I could, I would marry you, some day. But you must wait a while, and let me think.'

It was enough for him, and he was blithe at their parting. Not so she. To tell Randolph seemed impossible. She could wait till he had gone up to Oxford, when what she did would affect his life but little. But would he ever tolerate the idea? And if not, could she defy him?

She had not told him a word when the yearly cricket match came on at Lord's between the public schools, though Sam had already gone back to Aldbrickham. Mrs Twycott felt stronger than usual: she went to the match with Randolph, and was able to leave her chair and walk about occasionally. The bright idea occurred to her that she could casually broach the subject while moving round among the spectators, when the boy's spirits were high with interest in the game, and he would weigh domestic matters as feathers in the scale beside the day's victory. They promenaded under the lurid July sun, this pair, so wide apart, yet so near, and Sophy saw the large proportion of boys like her own, in their broad white collars and dwarf hats, and all around the rows of great coaches under which was jumbled the debris of luxurious luncheons; bones, pie-crusts, champagne-bottles, glasses, plates, napkins, and the family silver; while on the coaches sat the proud fathers and mothers; but never a poor mother like her. If Randolph had not appertained to these, had not centred all his interests in them, had not cared exclusively for the class they belonged to, how happy would things have been! A great huzza at some small performance with the bat burst from the multitude of relatives, and Randolph jumped wildly into the air to see what had happened. Sophy fetched up the sentence that had been already shaped; but she could not get it out. The occasion was, perhaps, an inopportune one. The contrast between her story and the display of fashion to which Randolph had grown to regard himself as akin would be fatal. She awaited a better time.

It was on an evening when they were alone in their plain suburban residence, where life was not blue but brown, that she ultimately broke silence, qualifying her announcement of a probable second marriage by assuring him that it would not take place for a long time to come, when he would be living quite independently of her.

The boy thought the idea a very reasonable one, and asked if she had chosen anybody? She hesitated; and he seemed to have a misgiving. He hoped his stepfather would be a gentleman? he said.

'Not what you call a gentleman,' she answered timidly. 'He'll be much as I was before I knew your father;' and by degrees she acquainted him with the whole. The youth's face remained fixed for a moment; then he flushed, leant on the table, and burst into passionate tears.

His mother went up to him, kissed all of his face that she could get at, and patted his back as if he were still the baby he once had been, crying herself the while. When he had somewhat recovered from his paroxysm he went hastily to his own room and fastened the door.

Parleyings were attempted through the keyhole, outside which she waited and listened. It was long before he would reply, and when he did it was to say sternly at her from within: 'I am ashamed of you! It will ruin me! A miserable boor! A churl! a clown! It will degrade me in the eyes of all the gentlemen of England!'

'Say no more—perhaps I am wrong! I will struggle against it!' she cried miserably.

Before Randolph left her that summer a letter arrived from Sam to inform her that he had been unexpectedly fortunate in obtaining the shop. He was in possession; it was the largest in the town, combining fruit with vegetables, and he thought it would form a home worthy even of her some day. Might he not run up to town to see her?

She met him by stealth, and said he must still wait for her final answer. The autumn dragged on, and when Randolph was home at Christmas for the holidays she broached the matter again. But the young gentleman was inexorable.

It was dropped for months; renewed again; abandoned under his repugnance; again attempted; and thus the gentle creature reasoned and pleaded till four or five long years had passed. Then the faithful Sam revived his suit with some peremptoriness. Sophy's son, now an undergraduate, was down from Oxford one Easter, when she again opened the subject. As soon as he was ordained, she argued, he would have a home of his own, wherein she, with her bad grammar and her ignorance, would be an encumbrance to him. Better obliterate her as much as possible.

He showed a more manly anger now, but would not agree. She on her side was more persistent, and he had doubts whether she could be trusted in his absence. But by indignation and contempt for her taste he completely maintained his ascendancy; and finally taking her before a little cross and altar that he had erected in his bedroom for his private devotions, there bade her kneel, and swear that she would not wed Samuel Hobson without his consent. 'I owe this to my father!' he said.

The poor woman swore, thinking he would soften as soon as he was ordained and in full swing of clerical work. But he did not. His education had by this time sufficiently ousted his humanity to keep him quite firm; though his mother might have led an idyllic life with her faithful fruiterer and greengrocer, and nobody have been anything the worse in the world.

Her lameness became more confirmed as time went on, and she seldom or never left the house in the long southern thoroughfare, where she seemed to be pining her heart away. 'Why mayn't I say to Sam that I'll marry him? Why mayn't I?' she would murmur plaintively to herself when nobody was near.

Some four years after this date a middle-aged man was standing at the door of the largest fruiterer's shop in Aldbrickham. He was the proprietor, but today, instead of his usual business attire, he wore a neat suit of black; and his window was partly shuttered. From the railway-station a funeral procession was seen approaching: it passed his door and went out of the town towards the village of Gaymead. The man, whose eyes were wet, held his hat in his hand as the vehicles moved by; while from the mourning coach a young smooth-shaven priest in a high waistcoat looked black as a cloud at the shopkeeper standing there.

7

FOR CONSCIENCE' SAKE

I

Whether the utilitarian or the intuitive theory of the moral sense be upheld, it is beyond question that there are a few subtle-souled persons with whom the absolute gratuitousness of an act of reparation is an inducement to perform it; while exhortation as to its necessity would breed excuses for leaving it undone. The case of Mr Millborne and Mrs Frankland particularly illustrated this, and perhaps something more.

There were few figures better known to the local crossing-sweeper than Mr Millborne's, in his daily comings and goings along a familiar and quiet London street, where he lived inside the door marked eleven, though not as householder. In age he was fifty at least, and his habits were as regular as those of a person can be who has no occupation but the study of how to keep himself employed. He turned almost always to the right on getting to the end of his street, then he went onward down Bond Street to his club, whence he returned by precisely the same course about six o'clock, on foot; or, if he went to dine, later on in a cab. He was known to be a man of some means, though apparently not wealthy. Being a bachelor he seemed to prefer his present mode of living as a lodger in Mrs Towney's best rooms, with the use of furniture which he had bought ten times over in rent during his tenancy, to having a house of his own.

None among his acquaintance tried to know him well, for his manner and moods did not excite curiosity or deep friendship. He was not a man who seemed to have anything on his mind, anything to conceal, anything to impart. From his casual remarks it was generally understood that he was country-born, a native of some place in Wessex; that he had come to London as a young man in a banking-house, and had risen to a post of responsibility; when, by the death of his father, who had been fortunate in his investments, the son succeeded to an income which led him to retire from a business life somewhat early.

One evening, when he had been unwell for several days, Doctor Bindon came in, after dinner, from the adjoining medical quarter, and smoked with him over the fire. The patient's ailment was not such as to require much thought, and they talked together on indifferent subjects.

'I am a lonely man, Bindon—a lonely man,' Millborne took occasion to say, shaking his head gloomily. 'You don't know such loneliness as mine... And the older I get the more I am dissatisfied with myself. And today I have been, through an accident, more than usually haunted by what, above all other events of my life, causes that dissatisfaction—the recollection of an unfulfilled promise made twenty years ago. In ordinary affairs I have always been considered a man of my word and perhaps it is on that account that a particular vow I once made, and did not keep, comes back to me with a magnitude out of all proportion (I daresay) to its real gravity, especially at this time of day. You know the discomfort caused at night by the half-sleeping sense that a door or window has been left unfastened, or in the day by the remembrance of unanswered letters. So does that promise haunt me from time to time, and has done today particularly.'

There was a pause, and they smoked on. Millborne's eyes, though fixed on the fire, were really regarding attentively a town in the West of England.

'Yes,' he continued, 'I have never quite forgotten it, though during the busy years of my life it was shelved and buried under the pressure of my pursuits. And, as I say, today in particular, an incident in the law-report of a somewhat similar kind has brought it back again vividly. However, what it was I can tell you in a few words, though no doubt you, as a man of the world, will smile at the thinness of my skin when you hear it... I came up to town at one-and-twenty, from Toneborough, in Outer Wessex, where I was born, and where, before I left, I had won the heart of a young woman of my own age. I promised her marriage, took advantage of my promise, and— am a bachelor.'

'The old story.'

The other nodded.

'I left the place, and thought at the time I had done a very clever thing in getting so easily out of an entanglement. But I have lived long enough for that promise to return to bother me—to be honest, not altogether as a pricking of the conscience, but as a dissatisfaction with myself as a specimen of the heap of flesh called humanity. If I were to ask you to lend me fifty pounds, which I would repay you next midsummer, and I did not repay you, I should consider myself a shabby sort of fellow, especially if you wanted the money badly. Yet I promised that girl just as distinctly; and then coolly broke my word, as if doing so were rather smart conduct than a mean action, for which the poor victim herself, encumbered with a child, and not I, had really to pay the penalty, in spite of certain pecuniary aid that was given. There, that's the retrospective trouble that I am always unearthing; and you may hardly believe that though so many years have elapsed, and it is all gone by and done with, and she must be getting on for an old woman now, as I am for an old man, it really often destroys my sense of self-respect still.'

'O, I can understand it. All depends upon the temperament. Thousands of men would have forgotten all about it; so would you, perhaps, if you had married and had a family. Did she ever marry?'

'I don't think so. O no—she never did. She left Toneborough, and later on appeared under another name at Exonbury, in the next county, where she was not known. It is very seldom that I go down into that part of the country, but in passing through Exonbury, on one occasion, I learnt that she was quite a settled resident there, as a teacher of music, or something of the kind. That much I casually heard when I was there two or three years ago. But I have never set eyes on her since our original acquaintance, and should not know her if I met her.'

'Did the child live?' asked the doctor.

'For several years, certainly,' replied his friend. 'I cannot say if she is living now. It was a little girl. She might be married by this time as far as years go.'

'And the mother—was she a decent, worthy young woman?'

'O yes; a sensible, quiet girl, neither attractive nor unattractive to the ordinary observer; simply commonplace. Her position at the time of our acquaintance was not so good as mine. My father was a solicitor, as I think I have told you. She was a young girl in a music-shop; and it was represented to me that it would be beneath my position to marry her. Hence the result.'

'Well, all I can say is that after twenty years it is probably too late to think of mending such a matter. It has doubtless by this time mended itself. You had better dismiss it from your mind as an evil past your control. Of course, if mother and daughter are alive, or either, you might settle something upon them, if you were inclined, and had it to spare.'

'Well, I haven't much to spare; and I have relations in narrow circumstances—perhaps narrower than theirs. But that is not the point. Were I ever so rich I feel I could not rectify the past by money. I did not promise to enrich her. On the contrary, I told her it would probably be dire poverty for both of us. But I did promise to make her my wife.'

'Then find her and do it,' said the doctor jocularly as he rose to leave.

'Ah, Bindon. That, of course, is the obvious jest. But I haven't the slightest desire for marriage; I am quite content to live as I have lived. I am a bachelor by nature, and instinct, and habit, and everything. Besides, though I respect her still (for she was not an atom to blame), I haven't any shadow of love for her. In my mind she exists as one of those women you think well of, but find uninteresting. It would be purely with the idea of putting wrong right that I should hunt her up, and propose to do it offhand.'

'You don't think of it seriously?' said his surprised friend.

'I sometimes think that I would, if it were practicable; simply, as I say, to recover my sense of being a man of honour.'

'I wish you luck in the enterprise,' said Doctor Bindon. 'You'll soon be out of that chair, and then you can put your impulse to the test. But—after twenty years of silence—I should say, don't!'

II

The doctor's advice remained counterpoised, in Millborne's mind, by the aforesaid mood of seriousness and sense of principle, approximating often to religious sentiment, which had been evolving itself in his breast for months, and even years.

The feeling, however, had no immediate effect upon Mr Millborne's actions. He soon got over his trifling illness, and was vexed with himself for having, in a moment of impulse, confided such a case of conscience to anybody.

But the force which had prompted it, though latent, remained with him and ultimately grew stronger. The upshot was that about four months after the date of his illness and disclosure, Millborne found himself on a mild spring morning at Paddington Station, in a train that was starting for the west. His many intermittent thoughts on his broken promise from time to time, in those hours when loneliness brought him face to face with his own personality, had at last resulted in this course.

The decisive stimulus had been given when, a day or two earlier, on looking into a Post-Office Directory, he learnt that the woman he had not met for twenty years was still living on at Exonbury under the name she had assumed when, a year or two after her disappearance from her native town and his, she had returned from abroad as a young widow with a child, and taken up her residence at the former city. Her condition was apparently but little changed, and her daughter seemed to be with her, their names standing in the Directory as 'Mrs Leonora Frankland and Miss Frankland, Teachers of Music and Dancing'.

Mr Millborne reached Exonbury in the afternoon, and his first business, before even taking his luggage into the town, was to find the house occupied by the teachers. Standing in a central and open place it was not difficult to discover, a well-burnished brass door-plate bearing their names prominently. He hesitated to enter without further knowledge, and ultimately took lodgings over a toy-shop opposite, securing a sitting-room which faced a similar drawing or sitting-room at the Franklands', where the dancing lessons were given. Installed here he was enabled to make indirectly, and without suspicion, inquiries and observations on the character of the ladies over the way, which he did with much deliberateness.

He learnt that the widow, Mrs Frankland, with her one daughter, Frances, was of cheerful and excellent repute, energetic and painstaking with her pupils, of whom she had a good many, and in whose tuition her daughter assisted her. She was quite a recognized townswoman, and though the dancing branch of her profession was perhaps a trifle worldly, she was really a serious-minded lady who, being obliged to live by what she knew how to teach, balanced matters by lending a hand at charitable bazaars, assisting at sacred concerts, and giving musical recitations in aid of funds for bewildering happy savages, and other such enthusiasms of this enlightened country. Her daughter was one of the foremost of the bevy of young women who decorated the churches at Easter and Christmas, was organist in one of those edifices, and had subscribed to the testimonial of a silver broth-basin that was presented to the Reverend Mr Walker as a token of gratitude for his faithful and arduous intonations of six months as sub-precentor in the Cathedral. Altogether mother and daughter appeared to be a typical and innocent pair among the genteel citizens of Exonbury.

As a natural and simple way of advertising their profession they allowed the windows of the music-room to be a little open, so that you had the pleasure of hearing all along the street at any hour between sunrise and sunset fragmentary gems of classical music as interpreted by the young people of twelve or fourteen who took lessons there. But it was said that Mrs Frankland made most of her income by letting out pianos on hire, and by selling them as agent for the makers.

The report pleased Millborne; it was highly creditable, and far better than he had hoped. He was curious to get a view of the two women who led such blameless lives.

He had not long to wait to gain a glimpse of Leonora. It was when she was standing on her own doorstep, opening her parasol, on the morning after his arrival. She was thin, though not gaunt; and a good, well-wearing, thoughtful face had taken the place of the one which had temporarily attracted him in the days of his nonage. She wore black, and it became her in her character of widow. The daughter next appeared; she was a smoothed and rounded copy of her mother, with the same decision in her mien that Leonora had, and a bounding gait in which he traced a faint resemblance to his own at her age.

For the first time he absolutely made up his mind to call on them. But his antecedent step was to send Leonora a note the next morning, stating his proposal to visit her, and suggesting the evening as the time, because she seemed to be so greatly occupied in her professional capacity during the day. He purposely worded his note in such a form as not to require an answer from her which would be possibly awkward to write.

No answer came. Naturally he should not have been surprised at this; and yet he felt a little checked, even though she had only refrained from volunteering a reply that was not demanded.

At eight, the hour fixed by himself, he crossed over and was passively admitted by the servant. Mrs Frankland, as she called herself, received him in the large music-and-dancing room on the first-floor front, and not in any private little parlour as he had expected. This cast a distressingly business-like colour over their first meeting after so many years of severance. The woman he had wronged stood before him, well-dressed, even to his metropolitan eyes, and her manner as she came up to him was dignified even to hardness. She certainly was not glad to see him. But what could he expect after a neglect of twenty years!

'How do you do, Mr Millborne?' she said cheerfully, as to any chance caller. 'I am obliged to receive you here because my daughter has a friend downstairs.'

'Your daughter—and mine.'

'Ah—yes, yes,' she replied hastily, as if the addition had escaped her memory. 'But perhaps the less said about that the better, in fairness to me. You will consider me a widow, please.'

'Certainly, Leonora...' He could not get on, her manner was so cold and indifferent. The expected scene of sad reproach, subdued to delicacy by the run of years, was absent altogether. He was obliged to come to the point without preamble.

'You are quite free, Leonora—I mean as to marriage? There is nobody who has your promise, or—'

'O yes; quite free, Mr Millborne,' she said, somewhat surprised.

'Then I will tell you why I have come. Twenty years ago I promised to make you my wife; and I am here to fulfil that promise. Heaven forgive my tardiness!'

Her surprise was increased, but she was not agitated. She seemed to become gloomy, disapproving. 'I could not entertain such an idea at this time of life,' she said after a moment or two. 'It would complicate matters too greatly. I have a very fair income, and require no help of any sort. I have no wish to marry... What could have induced you to come on such an errand now? It seems quite extraordinary, if I may say so!'

'It must—I daresay it does,' Millborne replied vaguely; 'and I must tell you that impulse—I mean in the sense of passion—has little to do with it. I wish to marry you, Leonora; I much desire to marry you. But it is an affair of conscience, a case of fulfilment. I promised you, and it was dishonourable of me to go away. I want to remove that sense of dishonour before I die. No doubt we might get to love each other as warmly as we did in old times?'

She dubiously shook her head. 'I appreciate your motives, Mr Millborne; but you must consider my position; and you will see that, short of the personal wish to marry, which I don't feel, there is no reason why I should change my state, even though by so doing I should ease your conscience. My position in this town is a respected one; I have built it up by my own hard labours, and, in short, I don't wish to alter it. My daughter, too, is just on the verge of an engagement to be married, to a young man who will make her an excellent husband. It will be in every way a desirable match for her. He is downstairs now.'

'Does she know—anything about me?'

'O no, no; God forbid! Her father is dead and buried to her. So that, you see, things are going on smoothly, and I don't want to disturb their progress.'

He nodded. 'Very well,' he said, and rose to go. At the door, however, he came back again.

'Still, Leonora,' he urged, 'I have come on purpose; and I don't see what disturbance would be caused. You would simply marry an old friend. Won't you reconsider? It is no more than right that we should be united, remembering the girl.'

She shook her head, and patted with her foot nervously.

'Well, I won't detain you,' he added. 'I shall not be leaving Exonbury yet. You will allow me to see you again?'

'Yes; I don't mind,' she said reluctantly.

The obstacles he had encountered, though they did not reanimate his dead passion for Leonora, did certainly make it appear indispensable to his peace of mind to overcome her coldness. He called frequently. The first meeting with the daughter was a trying ordeal, though he did not feel drawn towards her as he had expected to be; she did not excite his sympathies. Her mother confided to Frances the errand of 'her old friend', which was viewed by the daughter with strong disfavour. His desire being thus uncongenial to both, for a long time Millborne made not the least impression upon Mrs Frankland. His attentions pestered her rather than pleased her. He was surprised at her firmness, and it was only when he hinted at moral reasons for their union that she was ever shaken. 'Strictly speaking,' he would say, 'we ought, as honest persons, to marry; and that's the truth of it, Leonora.'

'I have looked at it in that light,' she said quickly. 'It struck me at the very first. But I don't see the force of the argument. I totally deny that after this interval of time I am bound to marry you for honour's sake. I would have married you, as you know well enough, at the proper time. But what is the use of remedies now?'

They were standing at the window. A scantly-whiskered young man, in clerical attire, called at the door below. Leonora flushed with interest.

'Who is he?' said Mr Millborne.

'My Frances's lover. I am so sorry—she is not at home! Ah! They have told him where she is, and he has gone to find her... I hope that suit will prosper, at any rate!'

'Why shouldn't it?'

'Well, he cannot marry yet; and Frances sees but little of him now he has left Exonbury. He was formerly doing duty here, but now he is curate of St. John's, Ivell, fifty miles up the line. There is a tacit agreement between them, but—there have been friends of his who object, because of our vocation. However, he sees the absurdity of such an objection as that, and is not influenced by it.'

'Your marriage with me would help the match, instead of hindering it, as you have said.'

'Do you think it would?'

'It certainly would, by taking you out of this business altogether.'

By chance he had found the way to move her somewhat, and

he followed it up. This view was imparted to Mrs Frankland's daughter, and it led her to soften her opposition. Millborne, who had given up his lodging in Exonbury, journeyed to and fro regularly, till at last he overcame her negations, and she expressed a reluctant assent.

They were married at the nearest church; and the goodwill—whatever that was—of the music-and-dancing connection was sold to a successor only too ready to jump into the place, the Millbornes having decided to live in London.

III

Millborne was a householder in his old district, though not in his old street, and Mrs Millborne and their daughter had turned themselves into Londoners. Frances was well reconciled to the removal by her lover's satisfaction at the change. It suited him better to travel from Ivell a hundred miles to see her in London, where he frequently had other engagements, than fifty in the opposite direction where nothing but herself required his presence. So here they were, furnished up to the attics, in one of the small but popular streets of the West district, in a house whose front, till lately of the complexion of a chimney-sweep, had been scraped to show to the surprised wayfarer the bright yellow and red brick that had lain lurking beneath the soot of fifty years.

The social lift that the two women had derived from the alliance was considerable; but when the exhilaration which accompanies a first residence in London, the sensation of standing on a pivot of the world, had passed, their lives promised to be somewhat duller than when, at despised Exonbury, they had enjoyed a nodding acquaintance with three-fourths of the town. Mr Millborne did not criticize his wife; he could not. Whatever defects of hardness and acidity his original treatment and the lapse of years might have developed in her, his sense of a realized idea, of a re-established self-satisfaction, was always thrown into the scale on her side, and out-weighed all objections.

It was about a month after their settlement in town that the household decided to spend a week at a watering-place in the Isle of Wight, and while there the Reverend Percival Cope (the young curate aforesaid) came to see them, Frances in particular. No formal engagement of the young pair had been announced as yet, but it was clear that their mutual understanding could not end in anything but marriage without grievous disappointment to one of the parties at least. Not that Frances was sentimental. She was rather of the imperious sort, indeed; and, to say all, the young girl had not fulfilled her father's expectations of her. But he hoped and worked for her welfare as sincerely as any father could do.

Mr Cope was introduced to the new head of the family, and stayed with them in the Island two or three days. On the last day of his visit they decided to venture on a two hours' sail in one of the small yachts which lay there for hire. The trip had not progressed far before all, except the curate, found that sailing in a breeze did not quite agree with them; but as he seemed to enjoy the experience, the other three bore their condition as well as they could without grimace or complaint, till the young man, observing their discomfort, gave immediate directions to tack about. On the way back to port they sat silent, facing each other.

Nausea in such circumstances, like midnight watching, fatigue, trouble, fright, has this marked effect upon the countenance, that it often brings out strongly the divergences of the individual from the norm of his race, accentuating superficial peculiarities to radical distinctions. Unexpected physiognomies will uncover themselves at these times in well-known faces; the aspect becomes invested with the spectral presence of entombed and forgotten ancestors; and family lineaments of special or exclusive cast, which in ordinary moments are masked by a stereotyped expression and mien, start up with crude insistence to the view.

Frances, sitting beside her mother's husband, with Mr Cope opposite, was naturally enough much regarded by the curate during the tedious sail home; at first with sympathetic smiles. Then, as the middle-aged father and his child grew each greyfaced, as the pretty blush of Frances disintegrated into spotty stains, and the soft rotundities of her features diverged from their familiar and reposeful beauty into elemental lines, Cope was gradually struck with the resemblance between a pair in their discomfort who in their ease presented nothing to the eye in common. Mr Millborne and Frances in their indisposition were strangely, startlingly alike.

The inexplicable fact absorbed Cope's attention quite. He forgot to smile at Frances, to hold her hand; and when they touched the shore he remained sitting for some moments like a man in a trance.

As they went homeward, and recovered their complexions and contours, the similarities one by one disappeared, and Frances and Mr Millborne were again masked by the commonplace differences of sex and age. It was as if, during the voyage, a mysterious veil had been lifted, temporarily revealing a strange pantomime of the past.

During the evening he said to her casually: 'Is your stepfather a cousin of your mother, dear Frances?'

'Oh, no,' said she. 'There is no relationship. He was only an old friend of hers. Why did you suppose such a thing?'

He did not explain, and the next morning started to resume his duties at Ivell.

Cope was an honest young fellow, and shrewd withal. At

home in his quiet rooms in St. Peter's Street, Ivell, he pondered long and unpleasantly on the revelations of the cruise. The tale it told was distinct enough, and for the first time his position was an uncomfortable one. He had met the Franklands at Exonbury as parishioners, had been attracted by Frances, and had floated thus far into an engagement which was indefinite only because of his inability to marry just yet. The Franklands' past had apparently contained mysteries, and it did not coincide with his judgment to marry into a family whose mystery was of the sort suggested. So he sat and sighed, between his reluctance to lose Frances and his natural dislike of forming a connection with people whose antecedents would not bear the strictest investigation.

A passionate lover of the old-fashioned sort might possibly never have halted to weigh these doubts; but though he was in the church Cope's affections were fastidious—distinctly tempered with the alloys of the century's decadence. He delayed writing to Frances for some while, simply because he could not tune himself up to enthusiasm when worried by suspicions of such a kind.

Meanwhile the Millbornes had returned to London, and Frances was growing anxious. In talking to her mother of Cope she had innocently alluded to his curious inquiry if her mother and her stepfather were connected by any tie of cousinship. Mrs Millborne made her repeat the words. Frances did so, and watched with inquisitive eyes their effect upon her elder.

'What is there so startling in his inquiry then?' she asked. 'Can it have anything to do with his not writing to me?'

Her mother flinched, but did not inform her, and Frances also was now drawn within the atmosphere of suspicion. That night when standing by chance outside the chamber of her parents she heard for the first time their voices engaged in a sharp altercation.

The apple of discord had, indeed, been dropped into the house of the Millbornes. The scene within the chamber-door was Mrs Millborne standing before her dressing-table, looking across to her husband in the dressing-room adjoining, where he was sitting down, his eyes fixed on the floor.

'Why did you come and disturb my life a second time?' she harshly asked. 'Why did you pester me with your conscience, till I was driven to accept you to get rid of your importunity? Frances and I were doing well: the one desire of my life was that she should marry that good young man. And now the match is broken off by your cruel interference! Why did you show yourself in my world again, and raise this scandal upon my hard-won respectability—won by such weary years of labour as none will ever know!' She bent her face upon the table and wept passionately.

There was no reply from Mr Millborne. Frances lay awake nearly all that night, and when at breakfast-time the next morning still no letter appeared from Mr Cope, she entreated her mother to go to Ivell and see if the young man were ill.

Mrs Millborne went, returning the same day. Frances, anxious and haggard, met her at the station.

Was all well? Her mother could not say it was; though he was not ill.

One thing she had found out, that it was a mistake to hunt up a man when his inclinations were to hold aloof. Returning with her mother in the cab Frances insisted upon knowing what the mystery was which plainly had alienated her lover. The precise words which had been spoken at the interview with him that day at Ivell Mrs Millborne could not be induced to repeat; but thus far she admitted, that the estrangement was fundamentally owing to Mr Millborne having sought her out and married her.

'And why did he seek you out—and why were you obliged

to marry him?' asked the distressed girl. Then the evidences pieced themselves together in her acute mind, and, her colour gradually rising, she asked her mother if what they pointed to was indeed the fact. Her mother admitted that it was.

A flush of mortification succeeded to the flush of shame upon the young woman's face. How could a scrupulously correct clergyman and lover like Mr Cope ask her to be his wife after this discovery of her irregular birth? She covered her eyes with her hands in a silent despair.

In the presence of Mr Millborne they at first suppressed their anguish. But by and by their feelings got the better of them, and when he was asleep in his chair after dinner Mrs Millborne's irritation broke out. The embittered Frances joined her in reproaching the man who had come as the spectre to their intended feast of Hymen, and turned its promise to ghastly failure.

'Why were you so weak, mother, as to admit such an enemy to your house—one so obviously your evil genius—much less accept him as a husband, after so long? If you had only told me all, I could have advised you better! But I suppose I have no right to reproach him, bitter as I feel, and even though he has blighted my life for ever!'

'Frances, I did hold out; I saw it was a mistake to have any more to say to a man who had been such an unmitigated curse to me! But he would not listen; he kept on about his conscience and mine, till I was bewildered, and said Yes!... Bringing us away from a quiet town where we were known and respected—what an ill-considered thing it was! O the content of those days! We had society there, people in our own position, who did not expect more of us than we expected of them. Here, where there is so much, there is nothing! He said London society was so bright and brilliant that it would be like a new world. It may be to those who are in it; but what is that to us two lonely women;

we only see it flashing past!... O the fool, the fool that I was!'

Now Millborne was not so soundly asleep as to prevent his hearing these animadversions that were almost execrations, and many more of the same sort. As there was no peace for him at home, he went again to his club, where, since his reunion with Leonora, he had seldom if ever been seen. But the shadow of the troubles in his household interfered with his comfort here also; he could not, as formerly, settle down into his favourite chair with the evening paper, reposeful in the celibate's sense that where he was his world's centre had its fixture. His world was now an ellipse, with a dual centrality, of which his own was not the major.

The young curate of Ivell still held aloof, tantalizing Frances by his elusiveness. Plainly he was waiting upon events. Millborne bore the reproaches of his wife and daughter almost in silence; but by degrees he grew meditative, as if revolving a new idea. The bitter cry about blighting their existence at length became so impassioned that one day Millborne calmly proposed to return again to the country; not necessarily to Exonbury, but, if they were willing, to a little old manor-house which he had found was to be let, standing a mile from Mr Cope's town of Ivell.

They were surprised, and, despite their view of him as the bringer of ill, were disposed to accede. 'Though I suppose,' said Mrs Millborne to him, 'it will end in Mr Cope's asking you flatly about the past, and your being compelled to tell him; which may dash all my hopes for Frances. She gets more and more like you every day, particularly when she is in a bad temper. People will see you together, and notice it; and I don't know what may come of it!'

'I don't think they will see us together,' he said; but he entered into no argument when she insisted otherwise. The removal was eventually resolved on; the town-house was disposed of; and again came the invasion by furniture-men and vans, till all the movables and servants were whisked away. He sent his wife and daughter to an hotel while this was going on, taking two or three journeys himself to Ivell to superintend the refixing, and the improvement of the grounds. When all was done he returned to them in town.

The house was ready for their reception, he told them, and there only remained the journey. He accompanied them and their personal luggage to the station only, having, he said, to remain in town a short time on business with his lawyer. They went, dubious and discontented— for the much-loved Cope had made no sign.

'If we were going down to live here alone,' said Mrs Millborne to her daughter in the train; 'and there was no intrusive telltale presence!... But let it be!'

The house was a lovely little place in a grove of elms, and they liked it much. The first person to call upon them as new residents was Mr Cope. He was delighted to find that they had come so near, and (though he did not say this) meant to live in such excellent style. He had not, however, resumed the manner of a lover.

'Your father spoils all!' murmured Mrs Millborne.

But three days later she received a letter from her husband, which caused her no small degree of astonishment. It was written from Boulogne.

It began with a long explanation of settlements of his property, in which he had been engaged since their departure. The chief feature in the business was that Mrs Millborne found herself the absolute owner of a comfortable sum in personal estate, and Frances of a life-interest in a larger sum, the principal to be afterwards divided amongst her children if she had any. The remainder of his letter ran as hereunder:

'I have learnt that there are some derelictions of duty which cannot be blotted out by tardy accomplishment. Our evil actions do not remain isolated in the past, waiting only to be reversed: like locomotive plants they spread and re-root, till to destroy the original stem has no material effect in killing them. I made a mistake in searching you out; I admit it; whatever the remedy may be in such cases it is not marriage, and the best thing for you and me is that you do not see me more. You had better not seek me, for you will not be likely to find me: you are well provided for, and we may do ourselves more harm than good by meeting again.

'F. M.'

Millborne, in short, disappeared from that day forward. But a searching inquiry would have revealed that, soon after the Millbornes went to Ivell, an Englishman, who did not give the name of Millborne, took up his residence in Brussels; a man who might have been recognized by Mrs Millborne if she had met him. One afternoon in the ensuing summer, when this gentleman was looking over the English papers, he saw the announcement of Miss Frances Frankland's marriage. She had become the Reverend Mrs Cope.

'Thank God!' said the gentleman.

But his momentary satisfaction was far from being happiness. As he formerly had been weighted with a bad conscience, so now was he burdened with the heavy thought which oppressed Antigone, that by honourable observance of a rite he had obtained for himself the reward of dishonourable laxity. Occasionally he had to be helped to his lodgings by his servant from the *Cercle* he frequented, through having imbibed a little too much liquor to be able to take care of himself. But he was harmless, and even when he had been drinking said little.

ABOUT TERRY O'BRIEN

Terry O'Brien is an academic with three decades of experience in teaching language and communication skills in India and abroad. He also headed a college under the auspices of the University of Delhi.

A prolific writer, with several books to his credit, Terry O'Brien is a reputed professional motivational speaker and a quizmaster.